"A lively and witty book. Have fun."
SSC Booknews

"Written low-keyed like a southern drawl, Crider depicts an assortment of characters that are genuine, diverse, and down home enough to want to make their aquaintance."
Mystery News

"Rhodes is a genuinely likable character. . . . Very enjoy-able."

Booklist

"Another agreeably folksy blend of pokey detection, lean action, and smalltown-Texas drollery."
The Kirkus Reviews

CURSED TO DEATH

Bill Crider

IVY BOOKS • NEW YORK

For Bob Crider—Mastermind

Ivy Books
Published by Ballantine Books
Copyright © 1988 by Bill Crider

Library of Congress Catalog Card Number: 87-21891

ISBN 0-8041-0424-7

This edition published by arrangement with Walker and Company

Manufactured in the United States of America

First Ballantine Books Edition: May 1990

Chapter 1

"WHAT DO YOU MEAN, there's no law against it?" Samuel A. Martin, DDS, was wrought up. His sharp-featured face was suffused with red, and his hands were clenched tight.

"I didn't say there was no law against it," Sheriff Dan Rhodes told him. "I said I'd never heard of it before. Maybe we could make a case for abusive language."

"Abusive language, my foot," Martin said, stomping for emphasis. "She put a curse on me! She threatened my life!"

"Well," Rhodes said, "I don't think we could say she actually threatened you."

Martin turned away. The two men were in what had been the kitchen of the small frame house he had converted into his dental offices. Rhodes was sitting in a vinyl-covered chair, leaning forward with his elbows on the formica top of the table. Martin was standing at the sink, looking out into the backyard.

"She threatened me," Martin said. He turned back to Rhodes and repeated the statement. "She threatened me."

1

"Let's go over it again," Rhodes said. "Do you remember her exact words?"

"Not her exact words, but pretty close," Martin said. "It was too long for me to remember the whole thing, and there were some funny names in there. But basically she said something about me getting sick, losing all my money, and having all my teeth fall out."

Rhodes tried not to smile. It wasn't a bad curse to put on a dentist, though, he thought. He remembered the dentist who had worked on his own teeth when he was a kid, Dr. Cranfill, who had been dead for some years now. "This won't hurt any more than a little sticker burr up on a sandy land hill," Dr. Cranfill would say. Then he would jab the needle in Rhodes's gum and merrily jiggle it around while he pumped in the novacain, or whatever it was he used to deaden the mouth. It always hurt a lot more than a sticker burr.

Those days were long past, though. All dentists now were painless, or so Rhodes had heard. He hadn't needed any fillings for a long time. "Why did she curse you?" he asked.

"It didn't have anything to do with my practice," Martin said, as if he had been reading Rhodes's thoughts. "She's been renting one of my houses."

"Houses," Rhodes said, leaning back from the table. "Which houses?"

"Rental property," Martin said. He was a tall man, at least six and a half feet, and very thin. As he crossed his arms and leaned back against the sink counter, he reminded Rhodes of a big white crane. "I bought some houses and fixed them up. It was a tax thing."

"What was wrong with the house?" Rhodes asked.

"There wasn't anything wrong," Martin said. "Not with the house, anyway. It was just that I was trying to get her to pay the rent."

"I guess that can be pretty upsetting to some people," Rhodes said. "She owe you much?"

"Three months." Martin was calming down now, and his color was returning to normal. He had unclenched his fists. "I let the first month slide, which I guess was a mistake. The second month I went out to talk to her and found out she had

2

a man living there with her. That was all right with me, rent was the same. But you'd think one of them could pay it, wouldn't you?''

"What about the third month?''

Martin looked sheepish and studied the floor, an unpleasant yellow tile that Rhodes didn't much like. "Uh, that's when I took the TV set,'' Martin finally said.

"Took the TV set?''

"Well, they wouldn't pay.'' Martin unfolded his arms in a sort of appeal for understanding. "So I took something of value to hold until I got the money.''

"She might have a better case against you than you have against her,'' Rhodes said.

"Well, it just wasn't fair,'' Martin said. "There they had that big, expensive TV set—a brand-new RCA, mind you, a console. With stereo. *I* don't have stereo.''

"Me neither,'' Rhodes said. Not that he cared, really. Most of the old movies he liked to watch were made long before stereo came along.

"Anyway,'' Martin said, "I gave it back.''

"When?''

"After she cursed me.''

Rhodes couldn't help himself this time. He smiled.

"It's not funny, Sheriff,'' Martin said.

"I know,'' Rhodes said. "Do you have any witnesses to all this?''

"Of course I do,'' Martin said. "That's what's so upsetting. That woman came right into the office, and then barged right on into Room I, where I was working on a cavity in Jennie Dunlap's incisor.''

"So Jennie Dunlap is a witness?''

"Yes, but she's gone. Everyone heard. My assistant, my hygienist, my receptionist. You can ask any of them.''

"I guess I'd better,'' Rhodes said.

"I've had to cancel the rest of my appointments for the day,'' Martin said. "This has been awful. If you could only have heard the way that woman talked. . . .''

"I'm sure it was bad,'' Rhodes said. "Why don't you send the receptionist back first?''

3

"All right," Martin said. He almost had to bend to get through the doorway.

Rhodes got up and looked out the window. All the grass was dead, killed in the last freeze. There was a big pecan tree, its branches whipping in the wind. Martin had done a good job on this house. It was tight and quiet. You'd never know what was going on outside, unless you looked.

The receptionist came in. She was dressed in black slacks and a multicolored striped blouse. Dentists' offices just weren't what they used to be. She also looked about fifteen years old. Rhodes had found that one of the distracting things about reaching middle age was that everyone looked younger than you. Dr. Martin, for that matter, looked about twenty.

"I'm Sheriff Rhodes," he told the receptionist.

"I'm Tammy Green," she said. At least she didn't sound like a fifteen-year-old.

"Tell me about what happened this morning, Tammy," Rhodes said.

"O.K.," she said. "Can I sit down?"

"Of course."

She sat in the chair Rhodes had just left, then smiled at him. He could see why Martin had hired her. Either her family had spent a small fortune on orthodonic work, or she had naturally straight white teeth. Either way, she would have been a reassuring sight for people in a dental office.

"You heard what happened out there today?" Rhodes asked her. Now he was leaning against the sink.

"Sure," she said. "It would've been hard to miss it."

"Why don't you tell me what happened."

"Well, that Betsy Higgins came in. She looked a sight, too. An old sweater that looked like her daddy must've owned it, and that long dress dragging the floor. I swear."

"She didn't have an appointment, I guess."

Tammy laughed. "She sure didn't. I tried to tell her that Dr. Martin was busy, but she just wouldn't listen. She went right through the door and jumped him out while he was doing a filling. I heard her going on in there, loud as could be."

4

Rhodes pushed away from the sink and walked over to the table. "Could you hear what she said?"

"It was something about Dr. Martin getting sick and his teeth all falling out. And she was putting a curse on him. She said stuff about Lucifer and all."

"What did Dr. Martin do?"

"Well, he got all upset, naturally. He told her that the TV set was here and that she could have it back. He got it out of the storeroom and carried it to her car. Carol had to help him. She's the hygienist. She's a pretty big girl."

Tammy was no china doll herself. The short sleeves of her blouse were tight around her round white arms.

"Do you believe in curses?" Rhodes asked her.

"Well, I don't know about that," Tammy said. "But that Betsy Higgins is a real witch. I heard her tell Dr. Martin so. I wouldn't want her putting any curse on me, I'll tell you that."

"I guess not," Rhodes said. He sent Tammy back to the front, then interviewed Carol Shamblin, the hygienist, who had straight blonde hair that looked as if someone had inverted a soupbowl over her head before giving her a haircut. She had pretty much the same story to tell, and so did Jamie Fox, the assistant.

After he had talked to them Rhodes called Dr. Martin back. "Why'd you give her the TV set back?" he asked.

"I thought I'd better. She was pretty upset." Martin gave Rhodes a hard look. "It wasn't that I believed the curse," he said.

"What about your rent money?"

"The check is in the mail," Martin said.

"You could have her evicted," Rhodes said.

"That's a lot of trouble. Besides, I really do believe she'll pay. It's not that she's a bad renter. I've never had any trouble from her, which is a lot more than I can say for some of my other tenants."

"I guess I'd better have a talk with her, though," Rhodes said. "We can't have people going around cursing our dentists. It's not good for the county."

Martin managed a smile. "I'm sorry I got so agitated. I

5

shouldn't even have called you. I don't really want her put in jail or anything like that, not now that I've had time to think about it."

"I'm not going to arrest her," Rhodes said. "I don't think we have any witchcraft laws. I'll just talk to her, ask her to be a little better behaved in public. Maybe I'll even mention that the Sheriff's department can be called in to evict her, just in case that check isn't really in the mail."

"I'd appreciate that, Sheriff," Martin said. He put out his hand to be shaken. "She lives on Taylor Street. Two-twelve Taylor Street."

Rhodes took the hand, trying not to worry about how many mouths it had been in that day. "Give me a call if she causes you any more trouble."

"Thanks, Sheriff, I'll do that," Martin said.

Rhodes went out through the waiting room. There were comfortable-looking chairs, and on the wall there were signs saying "We Cater to Cowards" and "Did You Remember to Floss Today?" He felt vaguely guilty. To tell the truth, he couldn't remember having flossed in a week or two. Well, he'd do it tonight. He took his jacket off the old-fashioned coatrack and went outside.

When Rhodes was young he had seen comic postcards that depicted a map of Texas with the Panhandle stretching all the way to the North Pole. Only a single strand of barbed wire separated the two regions. On days like this he knew what the inspiration for the drawing was. It was December 3, and early in the morning a blue norther had come roaring down out of the high plains, dropping the temperature into the teens. It had warmed up a little, probably into the upper twenties, but that thirty-mile-an-hour wind went right through your clothes and directly to the bone. The sky was a solid gray overcast, and a little snow wouldn't have surprised Rhodes. It never stayed cold for too long in Blacklin County, but when it got cold, it got *cold*.

Rhodes got in the county car, started it, and turned on the heater. Cold air blew out on his feet. It would take a while to warm up, probably about as long as it would take him to drive over to Taylor Street.

Dr. Martin's rental property, at least this particular house, was not in the very best part of Clearview, the largest town in Blacklin County. The street was paved, but it hadn't been resurfaced recently, if you defined recently as any time within the last thirty years. It was full of potholes that were several feet wide, though not too deep. In places the paving had almost disappeared.

The houses that lined both sides of the street were mostly wood-frame structures in various states of disrepair. Here and there would be one with a fairly fresh coat of white paint, standing out the more prominently because of the contrast with the neighbors, which often had patched or peeling walls, screens hanging loosely, and an old truck seat on the front porch for a lounge chair.

Rhodes stopped in front of 212. It was one of the better ones; Dr. Martin hadn't been exaggerating when he said he'd fixed it up. The paint was no more than a year old, the screens were new, and there was even a sturdy cyclone fence.

The heater had just begun to warm Rhodes's feet. He hated to get out and face the wind again, but he did, hurrying up a narrow cement walk that was also new to knock at the door.

He tried not to shiver as he waited for someone to come to the door. Looking down at the porch, he saw that several of the boards in it had been replaced, though it had not been repainted.

The inner door opened, and looking through the screen Rhodes saw a man so big he looked as if he'd have to step through the door sideways to get out.

"Yeah?" the man said. He had a bass voice that one of the Oak Ridge Boys would have envied.

"I'm Sheriff Dan Rhodes," Rhodes said. "I'd like to talk to Betsy Higgins."

"If it's about that pansy dentist that took our TV, she ain't got nothin' to say." The man's voice rumbled up from the deep cavern of his chest, which seemed to act like his own private echo chamber.

"She's the one to tell me that," Rhodes said.

"Oh, hell, all right," the man said. He reached out a hand that you could lose a basketball in and opened the door.

7

Rhodes stepped inside, glad to get out of the wind and cold. The house, however, was unpleasantly warm.

"My name's Swan," the man said. "Phil Swan." He didn't offer to shake hands, for which Rhodes was grateful. "I'll get Betsy."

He went through a doorway at the back of the room, and Rhodes looked around. Martin had apparently furnished his rental houses, at least this one, with items he picked up at garage sales. There was an old floral couch with sagging cushions, a platform rocker with the patterned cover so worn that the foam rubber showed through, a coffee table with the varnish worn off three of the legs, and a what-not shelf that listed slightly to the left. There weren't any what-nots on it, just a couple of issues of *Prevention*, which Rhodes thought pretty strange reading for a witch.

Betsy Higgins came into the room. Swan was right behind her. She was wearing pretty much the same outfit Tammy had described, a bulky cable-knit sweater and a long black skirt that dragged the floor. The only thing that surprised Rhodes was her size. She looked like she might just be able to stand in Swan's hand, being no more than five feet tall, if that, and thin as a tenpenny nail.

"What can I do for you, Sheriff?" she asked. Her voice was thin and whiny.

"Where's your TV set?" Rhodes asked.

"It's in the bedroom," Swan said. "That's where we like to watch."

Rhodes wondered if Swan had had any trouble carrying the set in from the car. He didn't think so. "That's good," he said. "Miz Higgins, I've got to ask you about what happened down at Dr. Martin's office."

"I demanded my TV set back," she said. "He had no right to take it—"

"Damn straight," Swan said. "He tries anything like that again, I'm gonna wring his pipsqueak neck."

He flexed his huge hands. Rhodes didn't have any doubt he could do what he said. Probably wouldn't have to use more than his thumb and first finger, if Rhodes recalled Martin's neck rightly.

"I'm sure we can settle things a little more calmly than that," Rhodes said. "I understand you folks are a little behind in the rent."

"Don't matter," Swan said. "He ain't got no right to come in and take folks' belongings away. That's . . . stealing."

"He might think that failure to pay the rent is a little like stealing, too," Rhodes said.

Swan raised his hands and clenched them, as if he'd like to wring Rhodes's pipsqueak neck right then. Rhodes tried not to step backward.

"We'll pay," Betsy Higgins said. "I told him we'll pay."

"You know how some people are," Rhodes said. "They like to see the color of your money."

"I told him," Betsy said.

"Now about what else you told him . . ." Rhodes said.

"I didn't tell him anything else," she said.

"Now, Miz Higgins," Rhodes said. "Everybody in the office has a different story from that."

"You sayin' you don't believe her?" Swan asked, stepping forward lightly, balancing on the balls of his feet like an athlete.

Rhodes held his ground. "I'm saying that there are four or five witnesses who don't agree with her."

"Maybe they're lyin'." Swan's face was hard and weathered. He'd done a lot of outside work at one time or another. His coarse black hair looked as if he'd combed it with his fingers.

"I don't think they'd lie about something like this," Rhodes said. "I'd like to hear what Miz Higgins has to say."

"Oh, all right." Her own hair was stringy and brown, with a few streaks of gray. "I may have put a curse on him."

" 'May have'?" Rhodes said.

"I'm not sure. Sometimes when I get mad, I do things like that. I don't really mean anything by it."

"It sounded pretty serious to Dr. Martin," Rhodes said. "Serious enough for him to call the law."

"That skinny little . . ." Whatever else Swan had wanted to say was lost in a deep growl.

"It's all right, Phillip," Betsy said, laying a hand on his

9

huge arm. Then she turned to Rhodes. "I didn't give him a really severe curse, you know."

"Not really," Rhodes said.

"I cast a minor spell on him. It's all in the mind, really. The power of suggestion. If he's got a strong mind, he'll be all right."

Rhodes had an idea of what she meant. She didn't seem to have very much faith in her own magical powers, or whatever they were. If Martin believed she could put a curse on him, then he might be affected, but Rhodes couldn't see him being seriously hurt.

"All the same," he said after he'd thought about it, "it might be better if you avoided cursing people—or putting spells on them—around here. It might get you into trouble."

"As long as he stays out of my house," she said.

"As far as that goes," Rhodes said, "you'd better pay the rent. I'd hate to have to come back here to serve an eviction notice."

"Damn right, you'd hate it," Swan said. "You'd hate it so bad . . ."

Once more Betsy Higgins laid a hand on his arm. "We'll pay, Sheriff. Is that all you wanted to know?"

"I guess it is," Rhodes said. "Thanks for your time."

He turned and went back outside into the cold.

Chapter 2

SOMETIMES ON A SLOW DAY Rhodes liked to slip home in the middle of the afternoon and watch the Million Dollar Movie, but today he thought he'd better check in at the jail. He didn't like to talk much on the radio, since practically everybody in the county had a Radio Shack police scanner and had learned all the codes. Besides, he didn't know if there *was* a code for witchcraft.

The jail was old, but at least it was warm. In the office section, at any rate. The cells sometimes got uncomfortable, but Lawton, the jailer, provided prisoners with extra blankets at night if they asked for them.

When Rhodes walked in, Lawton and Hack Jensen, the dispatcher, were discussing the weather.

"I wish this wind would lay," Hack said.

"So do I," Lawton said. "We could use the eggs."

The two old men wheezed with laughter, and Rhodes joined in, not because the joke was funny but because it was so old. He had heard them use it a thousand times, but it never seemed to fail to tickle them.

Or maybe they just told it to aggravate him. He was never

11

quite sure. They both knew that they were indispensable to the county, working for next to nothing just so they would have something to do. Both were long past retirement age, but Lawton was a certified jailer, and Jensen kept things under control while the sheriff was out, taking calls and seeing that something was done about them.

They were complete opposites in appearance, Jensen tall and thin, Lawton short and stout, and one of their chief pleasures was withholding as much information from Rhodes as they could, right up until he would be almost about to lose his temper.

He knew the game, and they played it expertly. Usually he just went along with it, thinking of them as a comedy team. If Bob Hope and George Burns could do it at their ages, why not Jensen and Lawton?

Rhodes told them briefly about the Martin episode. "Either of you ever heard anything about him or that Betsy Higgins?"

"Never heard of her," Hack said. "I've heard a little about that tooth dentist, though."

"Me, too," Lawton said.

Rhodes didn't say anything. He knew better than to push them. It only made them worse.

The two old men looked at one another, as if deciding who would get to tell. It was usually Hack, and this time was no exception. "That little old house on Taylor Street ain't the only property he owns, not by a long shot."

"That's right," Lawton said. He brushed at his thinning hair as he spoke. Until very recently it had still had a few streaks of brown in it, but it was totally white now. "And that business with the TV? That's not the first time something like that's happened."

It was always a surprise to Rhodes that these two knew a lot more of the county gossip than he did, despite the fact that they were hardly ever out of the jail. Maybe people just talked more freely to them than they did to the sheriff.

"No, sir," Hack said. "Not the first time."

They looked expectantly at Rhodes. He looked back. He

12

thought of two old tomcats, one stringy and one hefty, look-ing at a bowl of food after a couple of days going hungry.

Finally Hack said, "Hear he like to've got into a fight a time or two with Little Barnes."

"Big Barnes, too," Lawton said. "Big Barnes said he'd whip Dr. Martin's butt so bad he'd have to stand up to sleep."

Big Barnes was Little Barnes's father, and both of them were known to be rowdy. In fact, both of them had been inside the jail a time or two, though no charges had ever been filed.

"Little Barnes rents that old Williams place out at Mt. Roma," Hack said. "Been runnin' a few cows on it, growin' a little garden. I hear he does all right, but he ain't gettin' rich. Maybe not rich enough to pay the rent every month."

"So he had a run-in with Dr. Martin?" Rhodes asked.

"That's what I hear," Lawton said. "Dr. Martin went out there to collect and kind of got ugly about it. Big Barnes was there helpin' Little Barnes do some work on the fence. I think it was in the lease that Little Barnes was supposed to keep up the fence. Anyway, there was a pretty good row about it."

"When did all this happen?" Rhodes asked.

"Month or so back," Hack said.

"That's all you know?"

"That's it," Hack said. "We don't gossip around here much."

"Too much work to do," Lawton said. "Keepin' these cells clean and all that."

"Right," Rhodes said. "Anything happen while I was out?"

"We had this runaway case," Lawton said.

Hack looked at him. He felt that, as dispatcher, it was his right to relate all the day's events, even if he'd already told Lawton about them.

"I think I better go sweep the cells again," Lawton said, but he didn't make any move to leave.

"It was a Miz Moffatt that called from out by Milsby," Hack said. He stopped and waited for Rhodes to ask for more.

13

Rhodes sighed. "I take it she wasn't the one who ran away."

"Didn't say anybody ran away," Hack said.

Rhodes looked accusingly at Lawton. Set up again.

"I said it was a runaway case," Lawton said. "Didn't say anybody had done any runnin'."

"I see," Rhodes said. He didn't, though.

"See, it's this Miz Moffatt's daughter that *wants* to run away," Hack said. "Ruby, her name is. Ruby Moffatt," he added helpfully.

Rhodes had it figured out. "She wants us to keep her daughter from running off, right?"

"Not exactly," Hack said.

Rhodes, who had been standing all this time, suddenly felt tired. He walked over to his desk and sat in the wooden chair. "What, exactly, did she want, then?"

"Her daughter, that Ruby, keeps threatenin' to run away and go live with her daddy. He's been separated from Miz Moffatt about three years now, got himself a cabin down by the Lake."

Rhodes knew that the Lake was Blacklin Lake in the southern part of the county. "She wants us to call the father and see if he'll take his daughter, then. If and when she runs away, I mean." It was a situation that arose every now and then, certainly nothing new.

"It ain't that," Hack said.

"See, the way it is—" Lawton started, but he hushed up when he saw Hack's glare.

"The way it is," Hack said, turning away from Lawton and looking at Rhodes, "the way it is, she wants to know if we'll provide an officer and a car for her. For Ruby, I mean."

"What?" Rhodes said. He sat up straight in the chair.

"That's exactly what I said," Hack told him. "I said, 'What?' "

"And what did she say?" Rhodes asked.

"She said Ruby didn't have a car. Said they'd tried to get her one of them hardship licenses, since she ain't but four-teen, but Ruby had some trouble passin' the test."

Rhodes thought instantly that Ruby must not be extremely

14

bright, since some of the questions on the reading portion of the Texas Driver's Test had always seemed to him designed for anyone to pass. Or at least anyone with any sense at all.

"So since Ruby didn't have a car . . ." Rhodes said.

". . . Miz Moffatt thought we might give her a ride," Lawton said. Then he was out the door leading to the cells quicker than any man his age had any right to move.

Hack had come halfway out of his chair, but he settled back down. It always irritated him when Lawton got the punch line. "Yeah," he said. "Miz Moffatt would sort of *like* for Ruby to run away, is the way I get it. 'Nothin' but trouble,' I think she said."

"So old dad gets her back, and everybody lives happily ever after," Rhodes said.

"That's right," Hack agreed. "Just like in *Cinderella*."

"Sure," Rhodes said. "It always works like that." He looked around the office, his eyes lighting on the gunrack. "Anybody cleaned those rifles and shotguns lately?"

"Not me," Hack said. "Ain't part of my job description."

"Right," Rhodes said. He knew who would have to clean the guns. They didn't get used very often, and he liked to keep them in good working order in case of emergency. Come to think of it, he couldn't recall just when the last emergency had been. Blacklin County covered a little over a thousand square miles, but was home to only around twenty thousand people. Crime there was not exactly rampant, and big-time crime was only something people learned about on TV.

"Any other calls?" Rhodes asked.

"Not that amount to nothin'," Hack said. "The usual things, cows in the wrong patch, dogs scarin' the neighbor's kids."

"Buddy and Ruth called in?"

"They haven't had much to say. Patrol must be pretty quiet today. It's Wednesday, after all."

Hack was right; Wednesday was usually the quietest day of the week. After that, people started gathering their energy for the weekend, and things would get busier.

15

"I think I'll go home and check on the dog," Rhodes said. "Call me if anything comes up."

"I'll do that," Hack said.

A couple of months before Rhodes had picked up Speedo, whose real name was Mr. Earl, while working on the murder of a man who had turned out to be an undercover drug agent. It wasn't that Rhodes had wanted a dog. It was just that he couldn't stand by and see one abandoned.

Rhodes pulled up at his house and parked. The pecan tree, like the one behind Dr. Martin's office, had lost most of its leaves, though a few thin brown stragglers still clung to the nearly bare branches. The wind was doing its best to tear them off. When Rhodes stepped out of the car, he crunched a pecan underfoot. He had picked up most of them as they had fallen, but some always managed to elude him. He moved his foot and looked down, but the nut was too mashed to bother with.

Speedo was in the backyard, pretty well sheltered from the wind in his new doghouse. It wasn't a house, exactly, but it served the purpose. It was an old fifty-five-gallon drum that Rhodes had gotten from a local gasoline distributor and filled with hay that he'd bought at a feed store. All in all, it was a pretty comfortable place for a dog to lie up and stay warm.

When Rhodes walked into the backyard, Speedo raised his head and looked at him, but made no offer to move out of the barrel. Rhodes didn't blame him. Speedo was at least some part collie and had a pretty thick coat of hair, but the way the wind was blowing hair didn't help much. Rhodes still had a fairly thick head of hair himself, but his head was so cold that he wished he was wearing a hat. Then he thought how he looked with a hat on, and decided that it was just as well he was bareheaded.

"You hungry, boy?" he asked the dog.

Speedo showed no interest in the query, putting his head back down on his paws.

Rhodes checked the food dish. It was nearly empty, so he got the sack of Old Roy out of the garage and put some in the dish. Speedo still didn't move. Rhodes took the sack back in the garage, and then looked at the water dish. The water was frozen.

"I'll get you some fresh water," he said. He hoped the hydrant would work. He had wrapped it with newspapers and burlap a few days ago. He turned the handle and water came out. He knocked the ice out of the bowl and let the fresh water run in. It was so cold that his hand felt frozen when he sloshed a little on it.

He set the dish down. "Better drink it while you can," he said.

Speedo didn't bother to look up.

Rhodes looked at his hands. They were red with cold. He thought he might look for his gloves before going back out. "See you later," he called to the dog, then went on into the house.

Rhodes didn't have central heating, but he had left all the natural gas space heaters on very low. It seemed quite warm in the house, but he knew it would seem cold if he stayed for very long.

He was tempted to go in and catch the end of the Million Dollar Movie, which he knew was *Walk the Proud Land* with Audie Murphy. Rhodes thought that Murphy was a vastly underrated actor, not that *Walk the Proud Land* was one of his better roles. One of these days, though, some critic was going to watch *The Quiet American* or *The Unforgiven*, and Audie would be rediscovered.

Instead of watching the movie, however, Rhodes walked into his bedroom. There it was, the new addition.

Standing not too far from his bed was a practically new Huffy Sunsprint stationary bicycle, which Rhodes had bought at a garage sale a week and a half before. Mr. Pollard, the former owner, swore that the mileage on the speedometer was the actual mileage (2153.3), and Rhodes had to admit that the bike was in excellent shape. Its sparkly brown paint didn't have a chip, and the white rubber wheel seemed not to be worn at all. It was a bargain at twenty dollars.

The mileage still hadn't changed. Rhodes looked at the machine at least once a day, and he really intended to get on

17

it and try it out soon, but somehow the right time never seemed to come.

He looked down at the floor. He could still see his feet. You certainly couldn't say he was fat, even if he couldn't quite see his belt buckle. Actually, he thought, he was in pretty good shape for a man of his age. He could still mix it up in a fight if he had to, as he had proved fairly recently. If he had to chase someone, he could do so without too much huffing and puffing.

On the other hand, no one would mistake him for Skinny Minnie, either. He had to admit that he had put on a few pounds in the last three or four years, part of the aging process, he supposed. He certainly hadn't changed his eating habits any. They were still bad.

Thinking of his eating habits led him to think of lunch. He had grabbed a hamburger before going to Dr. Martin's office, but that was all. Well, that and a Dr Pepper. One of these days, maybe he would think about diet drinks. But only as a last resort. He wondered if there was anything to eat in the refrigerator.

He went to look, mainly to get out of the room with the stationary bike. As he had suspected, there was nothing he wanted—the somewhat shriveled apple and the slightly off-color bologna held little appeal.

He walked into the living room and turned up the fire in the brown Dearborn heater. He would get started on his exercise program later. If Ivy Daniel really liked him, she liked him for what he was, and she wouldn't care if he carried a few extra pounds. He would have to ask her about that if the subject came up. They had been what Rhodes considered "sort of" engaged for several months now, and the subject shouldn't be embarrassing.

The problem was that Ivy wasn't carrying any extra weight around, and she was nearly as old as Rhodes.

Well, he thought, there's always the bicycle. He turned on the TV set to watch the last twenty minutes of *Walk the Proud Land*.

Chapter 3

DR. MARTIN DISAPPEARED a week and a half later.

His wife called Rhodes at home in the middle of the night, distraught. "I just can't understand it," she said. "He's never been away this late. Never! Not in the whole time we've been married. I just know something terrible has happened to him. You've got to find him, Sheriff!"

It was a Saturday night and Rhodes had been up very late. It was less than two weeks before Christmas, and the celebrating had already begun at various clubs and private parties around the county. Celebrating often led to drinking, which in turn often led to speeding, hazardous driving, accidents, and any number of other minor problems, all of which involved the Sheriff's Department. Rhodes was not at his best when awakened after only two hours' sleep.

He turned in the bed and looked at the clock, which to his gummy eyes seemed to say 3:13 in red digital letters. He lay back on the pillow. "Maybe he's just out getting in the Christmas spirit," he said.

"You haven't been listening, Sheriff," Mrs. Martin said.

She had a pleasant enough voice, but it definitely had an edge to it. "Sam would have told me if it had been anything like that. He has *never* stayed away without letting me know. I want you to find him."

"Do you have any idea where he might be?" Rhodes asked, still lying back in the bed.

"Not really. He left home around noon. He said he had to check up on some of his renters. He wanted to get the money they owed him before they spent it all on Christmas presents."

What a guy, Rhodes thought.

"Did he say which renters he was going to visit?" he asked.

"No," she said.

Great, Rhodes thought.

"I just know he's been in some horrible accident. He might be lying dead in a ditch right now," Mrs. Martin said. "And you've got to do something about it!"

Rhodes sat up. "I'll do what I can, Mrs. Martin, but I'll have to have some idea of where he might have gone. I can't just search the whole county at random. Do you have a list of the properties he owns and who owed him rent?"

"Of course," she said.

"I'll pick it up as soon as I can get dressed," Rhodes said.

"Thank you, Sheriff." Mrs. Martin hung up.

Rhodes sat with the phone in his hand for a minute, then forced himself to get out of the bed. The weather had been unusually warm for the past few days, almost like early fall, but the floor was still cold to his feet as he stepped on it.

He avoided the bicycle and stepped into the bathroom to splash some water on his face. It didn't really wake him up, but it seemed to help a little. It was too bad he didn't like coffee, he thought. Right now the caffeine rush would probably do him some good.

He dressed, slipped on a light nylon jacket, and went outside. It was a dark, almost cloudless night, crisp and cool. The sky was filled with stars. Rhodes looked up for a minute, almost glad that Mrs. Martin had called him.

Speedo padded over to see what was happening. Rhodes

knelt down and roughed his fur. Mrs. Martin could wait for a few more minutes. The more he thought about it, the more Rhodes was convinced that her husband had just gone out for a little holiday fun and would be back eventually. There didn't seem to be any need to hurry.

The Martins lived in what passed for opulence in most of Clearview. Their house was only five years old, and it sat on a large lot with several shade trees. There were only a few houses around it, most of them owned by lawyers, doctors, or other dentists. Clearview had three dentists, and all three lived within two blocks of one another.

The house was mostly brick, single story, and probably had over three thousand square feet of living space. It also had a four-car garage, and Rhodes could see as he pulled up to the side that only three vehicles were home: a Lincoln Town Car, which he assumed was Mrs. Martin's; a completely restored 1957 Chevrolet Bel-Air, white over green, which Rhodes wouldn't have minded owning himself; and a Toyota Camry. The fourth stall was empty, and Rhodes figured that Dr. Martin had been driving whatever had been parked there.

Rhodes walked past the open garage, to the front of the house. The porch was made of wide flat stones of varying sizes. Rhodes walked across it and rang the doorbell.

Almost immediately one of the double wooden doors was pulled open. "Come in, Sheriff," Mrs. Martin said. She was a short woman wearing a pale blue dressing gown of some shiny material that looked like silk but probably wasn't. The gown was belted tight around her waist. She had what Rhodes thought might be described as a "buxom" figure—wide hips and large breasts—but he almost caught himself staring at her hair, an old-fashioned bouffant style that was so stiff with spray that it looked as if you could crack pecans on it.

She didn't wait for Rhodes to come in, but turned and walked down the short entry hall to the den. Rhodes followed her. The den was about as big as Rhodes's whole house, divided into two sections by the arrangement of couches and chairs. In one corner was a Christmas tree that Rhodes was

21

sure had to be compressed to come in through the double door. The room's vaulted ceiling gave it plenty of room, however, even though it was at least nine feet tall. It was decorated entirely with red ornaments. The lights weren't on, but Rhodes thought that they would undoubtedly be red, too.

On the wall to Rhodes's right there was a built-in bookcase and home entertainment center. The bookshelves were not filled, but there were a few neatly arranged volumes. There was also a small desk. Mrs. Martin was standing by it.

"I have the information you wanted, Sheriff," she said. The edge was in her voice. "I hope I can count on you to check these places out."

"I will," Rhodes said, "but I can't guarantee that I'll find anything. For all we know, he might have gone somewhere that you don't have on the list."

"I'm sure that's possible," she said. She handed Rhodes a sheet of white paper. The list was neatly written in small rounded letters. There were four names.

"All of those people owed us rent," Mrs. Martin said. "I assume that he was going to see one or all of them."

Rhodes glanced at the list. Betsy Higgins, naturally. Little Barnes, too, along with Steve Reed and Harry Stokes.

"Do you, ah, know any of these folks?" Rhodes asked.

Mrs. Martin looked at him, her young face at complete odds with her dated hair-do. "If you mean that Higgins person, Sam has told me about the 'curse' she laid on him. Surely you don't think—"

"No, I don't," Rhodes said. "I don't put much stock in that sort of thing, myself."

Mrs. Martin clasped her arms beneath her breasts as if to hold them up. "I can assure you that I don't, either. And of course neither did Sam. Of course he was upset at first, but when he thought about it for a while, we both laughed."

"She's on the list, though," Rhodes said.

"Only because she still owes the rent she hadn't paid when she came into Sam's office and started cursing him," Mrs. Martin said. "It's only a coincidence."

"Well, I'll check it out," Rhodes said. "What I can do

tonight is drive around all these places, see if there's been an unreported accident. Make sure your husband didn't drive off in a ditch and get stuck. I really can't begin talking to people until daylight.''

"Why not?'' Her voice was sharp.

Rhodes answered softly because he could tell that she was genuinely worried. ''Because there hasn't been enough time for your husband to be an official 'missing person.' I can't go knocking on folks' doors in the middle of the night when he's only been gone a little over half a day. Tomorrow, when everybody's awake, I'll knock on doors.''

"Well . . . if that's the way it has to be done.'' She still wasn't happy. Rhodes thought that she was a woman used to getting her way.

"That's the way,'' he said. "But don't worry about it. He probably just had a flat, or engine trouble. Something like that. He'll be right here before daylight.'' He didn't mention what he really thought, that Dr. Martin was probably carousing somewhere.

"I hope you're right,'' Mrs. Martin said. "And you *will* check?''

"Of course,'' Rhodes said. "I'll get started right now.''

She showed him to the door.

As he stepped out, he turned. "What kind of car is he driving?'' It was the first thing he should have asked. He was sleepier than he had thought.

"Oh,'' Mrs. Martin said. "It isn't a car. It's a Chevrolet Suburban, a 1985. Solid black.''

"Do you know the license number?''

"It's a personalized plate,'' she said. Rhodes called them vanity plates. "It says 'TEETH.' ''

"Shouldn't be hard to spot,'' Rhodes said.

"No,'' she said. For the first time she almost smiled.

Rhodes drove through the downtown area just to see if anything was happening. Nothing was. The red and green tinsel hung limply from the light poles and the wires at the intersections, but the holiday lighting had been turned off. There was no traffic at all. All of the buildings were lighted

23

except the vacant ones, and there were too many of those. Rhodes could remember the time when everybody in Clearview, it seemed, was downtown on Saturday night, though of course not at this late hour. Now most of the stores closed at noon, and the town was dead and deserted by five o'clock. Everyone went to Wal-Mart.

After passing through town, Rhodes drove by the night-clubs on the outskirts of town. The Paragon. The Hot Club. The Club 44. All were closed, since it was now Sunday morning. Blacklin was what Rhodes called semi-dry. No liquor could be sold within the county's borders, either in bottles or by the drink, though beer and wine could be sold in grocery stores and in the clubs, which had been called honky-tonks in Rhodes's younger days. Some of the buildings had been around for at least that long, though there were newer ones like the Paragon that catered to the upscale crowd. The blue-collar drinkers liked it too, however.

No one had run a car in the ditches near any of the clubs. The area was completely deserted. Rhodes turned and drove toward Mt. Roma, a name he'd never quite understood. There was no mountain, and there was no resemblance to Rome. Maybe someone had just liked the name.

Rhodes wound among the peach orchards on the country road and soon came to Little Barnes's place, or the place he was renting from Dr. Martin. It was only about four miles from town, easy walking distance if anything had happened to a Suburban. The ditches were clear, and there were no signs of anyone's having driven off the dirt road. Rhodes went on by the Barnes place for about a half mile, but he found nothing. He was beginning to think that maybe Mrs. Martin was correct. Maybe something was wrong.

He drove back into town and by the house where Betsy Higgins lived. Parked beside it was a pickup he hadn't noticed before. In the back window was one of those diamond-shaped yellow signs with black lettering: "Bullrider on Board." There was no sign of the dentist's Suburban.

Steve Reed and Harry Stokes, the other two names on the list, were not familiar to Rhodes. He would have to wait until morning to check them out. He'd looked around, as he had promised. Now he was going to go home and sleep for a couple of hours. Or maybe three. He'd have to get up and catch everybody before church, except that he was pretty sure Betsy Higgins didn't go to church, being a witch, and he would be willing to bet that Little Barnes didn't go to church either. At least he didn't have the reputation of a church-going man. He didn't know about the others, though. Well, he could find out.

Rhodes got to the jail at nine o'clock, a little later than he had intended. He'd gotten home and made the mistake of turning on the TV just in time for a few minutes of *Untamed Women*, which was about a group of women druids who lived on a South Sea island. Rhodes didn't know just exactly how they had gotten there, and he never did find out before the volcano blew up at the end. He had been tempted once or twice to buy a video recorder, but he hadn't. He thought that to appreciate a movie like *Untamed Women* you had to watch it at around four-thirty in the morning with commercials for waterbed companies. So he'd overslept a little bit, despite his good intentions.

"I didn't expect to see you this morning," Hack said.

Rhodes told him about the disappearance of Dr. Martin.

"Ain't he the one got the curse put on him?"

"He's the one. I imagine he'll turn up, though. Probably out for a little Christmas cheer."

"We could use some of that around here," Hack said, looking around the office. "When all you got for decorations is Christmas cards from forensic labs, you ain't got much."

"Don't forget the one from Mrs. Wilkie," Rhodes said.

"She's not givin' up easy," Hack said. "She thinks she'll get you yet. You better watch your step."

"Don't worry," Rhodes said. "Anything happen last night that I should know about?"

"It was all quiet after you signed off," Hack told him.

Rhodes asked about Steve Reed and Harry Stokes.

"I'm not sure," Hack said. "Both of 'em rent out around Milsby, I think. Small places, not like the one Little Barnes has. They don't live there, though. They're just weekend

25

cowboys. Live in town and mess with cows in their spare time.''

"You mean I can look them up in the phone book," Rhodes said.

"If they got phones. We got a city directory, you know."

They were both in the phone book. "I'll check with you later," Rhodes said. "Give me a call if you need me."

"Always do," Hack said.

The sun was shining in an almost cloudless sky, and the temperature was nearly sixty degrees. Rhodes had a hard time believing that it was nearly Christmas. He wondered what he could get Ivy. He hadn't bought a gift for a woman for a while.

Neither Reed nor Stokes would admit to having seen Dr. Martin the previous day. Both in fact protested that their checks had been mailed, and Stokes even showed Rhodes the check stub. Reed was in a hurry to get to church, but he told Rhodes to come back later and he'd show him the records. Rhodes said he might not need to see them.

In fact, Rhodes was not a modern cop who believed in lie detectors, computers, and fancy interrogation methods. He relied on instinct and dogged investigation, asking questions until he got the right answers. He liked to think he was a good judge of people, though he would admit that he'd been fooled more than once. Anyway, his impression was that Stokes and Reed had nothing to hide.

So he drove to the house where Betsy Higgins and Phil Swan lived. The pickup was still there. Rhodes got out of his car and started walking to the door. Before he got there Swan shouldered his way outside.

"What's the trouble, Sheriff?" he asked.

"No trouble," Rhodes said. "I just wanted to talk to you and Miz Higgins again."

"What about?"

The house was up on blocks, and that made the porch where Swan was standing about a foot off the ground. He was already quite a bit taller than Rhodes, and now he looked down on him from an even greater height, glowering. He had a good face to glower with.

"Dr. Martin," Rhodes said.

"Well, we told you about that the other day," Swan said. "I don't know as we have any more to say."

"I don't think Dr. Martin ever got his money," Rhodes said. He didn't make any attempt to get up on the porch with Swan. There was room, but he didn't think he'd feel comfortable.

"Yeah, well the mail service is pretty bad these days," Swan said. "He'll get it sooner or later."

"I'm sure he will," Rhodes said. "Is that what you told him yesterday?"

"I don't know what you're talking about," Swan said.

"I'm talking about when he came to see you about the rent yesterday."

"We wasn't here yesterday," Swan said, his eyes looking vaguely off somewhere beyond Rhodes's head.

"So you didn't see Dr. Martin yesterday at all? Not here or anywhere else."

"That's right. Not here or anywhere." Swan was eager to agree. He leaned comfortably against the door frame now, relaxed.

"Well, that's all I really wanted to know," Rhodes said. "I may have to check back with you later, though."

"Sure, you do that," Swan said, grinning. He had big, square teeth.

"If the check doesn't get to Dr. Martin, I mean."

"Sure."

Rhodes went back to his car, not satisfied at all with what he'd heard. Still, the fact that he thought Swan was a liar didn't mean a thing. Not yet, anyway. He got in the car and drove away.

27

Chapter 4

ON HIS WAY to Little Barnes's place Rhodes stopped at the Dillie Gas & Gro. to use the pay phone. Dillie's was a little one-room wood-frame store of the kind that in Blacklin County could still compete with the more modern drive-ins. Dillie herself was behind the counter, as she always was. This time she was busily cutting out coupons from the advertising section of one of the Dallas Sunday papers.

Dillie looked up when Rhodes came through the door. "Hidy, Sheriff," she said. She had one of the deepest women's voices that Rhodes had ever heard. He was reminded of the kid actor "Foghorn" Winslow from thirty years before.

"Good morning," Rhodes said. He glanced down at the counter. It looked as if Dillie had taken the coupon sections out of every paper in the little red metal rack in front of the store. "I just need to use your pay phone."

"Sure, go ahead. Nobody in here but us." She looked down at the coupons in front of her, then glanced back up quickly. "I, ah, I was just clippin' these coupons out of the paper for my mother. She . . . she likes to use them when she shops for stuff I don't carry here."

Dillie was about forty years old, with very black hair that Rhodes suspected was kept that color with a little help from a dye bottle, but her skin was very white, as if she seldom went outside her little grocery. So her blush was even more evident than it might have been otherwise.

"I like to cut out a coupon every now and then, myself," Rhodes told her, heading for the phone on the wall. He knew very well that Dillie was going to send in those coupons herself. He couldn't imagine what possible use her mother could have for eight bottles of Gatorade. But if a crime was being committed, he didn't figure it was in his jurisdiction.

The pay phone was hanging on the wall by the side door, by shelves loaded with dusty cans of tomato sauce and Spaghetti-Os. The Clearview phone book was hanging by a dirty string tied to a nail driven into the wall. Rhodes looked up Martin's number and dialed. It was just possible that the dentist had showed up at home, and Mrs. Martin should be up by now in any case. It was nearly eleven o'clock.

Mrs. Martin answered on the first ring, and no, Dr. Martin had *not* come home, and Sheriff Rhodes had best get busy and find him before Mrs. Martin exercised some of her considerable power in the county—she knew several of the Commissioners personally, she said—to get someone in the Sheriff's office who knew what was happening in the world.

The woman sounded truly distracted, and Rhodes didn't hold what she said against her. In fact, he began to get a bit worried for the first time. It was looking as if Dr. Martin wasn't out on a binge after all. Instead of celebrating Christmas, maybe he really was in trouble. Rhodes wished he'd questioned Phil Swan a little more carefully. Well, he could always do it again, and make sure Betsy Higgins got in on it, too.

When he hung up the phone, he looked out the glass in the side door. Dillie sold minnows, which swam in a concrete tank, its water stirred by a small motor-driven blade.

"How much are minnows these days, Dillie?" he asked, turning back to the counter.

"Dollar seventy-five a dozen for the really good ones,"

she said. "Those big, frisky ones. You wouldn't want the others."

Rhodes hadn't been fishing in a long time, and most of the time he just had a few minutes to cast with artificial lures. He thought about the current warm spell. Maybe the bass would be biting. One of the biggest fish he'd ever caught had been taken on an H & H spinner on Thanksgiving Day, and it wasn't much after Thanksgiving now.

"Maybe I'll take a look at them," he said. "I don't have my minnow bucket with me right now."

"You just go ahead, Sheriff," Dillie said.

As Rhodes walked by the counter he saw that it had been cleared of coupons. "Thanks, Dillie," he said.

Outside he turned left and went around to the minnow tank. It was in an unheated wooden enclosure, and a lot of the minnows must have died of the cold lately. Dillie had cleaned most of them out, but two still floated belly up on the surface of the churning water. Rhodes scooped them out with his hand and tossed them outside. He took the dip net from the side of the tank, put it into the water, and brought out several of the shiners. They flipped and tossed, trying to get back in the water. Their backs were dark black and their sides shiny silver. Rhodes regretted that he never had time for fishing anymore. Maybe one day soon . . .

He turned the net over and tipped the minnows back into the water.

Little Barnes, whose real name was Harold, lived on the land he rented. The house was on top of a little rise about a quarter mile from the road. Rhodes had seen it but had never been inside.

He wouldn't have to go inside today, either, because Barnes was working close by the fence, digging postholes with a gasoline-powered auger.

Instead of a gate in the fence there was a cattle guard. Rhodes turned off the road and drove across the pipes that made up the cattle guard, his tires making a *b-r-r-a-a-p-p-ing* sound. Then he turned left and drove over to where Barnes was working.

30

Rhodes drove over to an old well house, which wasn't exactly a house but more of a roof over the round brick well. Someone had laid a square of concrete around the well, and the roof covered this also. Twenty or thirty yards away was a collapsing barn covered entirely in rusting sheet metal, most of which was barely clinging to the wooden frame, and some of which was lying on the ground. Looking toward the road, Rhodes could see at least one piece of it caught in the fence.

Growing beside the well house was a huge oak tree, or three of them growing out of one gigantic trunk. Rhodes stopped the car under the tree and got out.

Barnes shut off the auger and watched Rhodes walk toward him. He was called "Little" Barnes only to distinguish him from his father. He must have weighed in the vicinity of three hundred pounds, most of it fat. He had on a pair of Big Mac overalls that looked as if they could have served duty as a Cub Scout pup tent, and a red and black flannel shirt that could be used as a tarp for a baseball diamond. The sleeves of the shirt were rolled up, exposing Little's round arms, as big as many men's waists. Looking at him, Rhodes didn't feel so bad about not having begun his exercise program.

Barnes was not a clean person, as Rhodes well knew from the times both Little and Big had been guests of the county. Digging postholes was not clean work, but Barnes looked as if he hadn't bathed since 1982, or maybe as if he had been rolling in the soft, mucky earth under the remnants of the barn roof. His thin, lank black hair hung all around his face, partially hiding his small, piggy black eyes.

Rhodes stopped about ten feet from the man, but he could still smell him. "Pretty hot work, huh, Little?" he said.

Barnes grunted. "Not as bad as it used to be," he said.

He was right. Rhodes had dug a few postholes with the old-fashioned two-handled diggers himself years ago. Plunge the blades into the ground, squeeze the handles together, bring out the earth, and repeat the process until the hole was finished. You had to have strong hands, strong arms, and a strong back. Now you just had to have the weight to hold on

31

to the auger, and Barnes had that. If the ground was soft, the job was easy.

"What're you fixing to build?" Rhodes asked.

"Corral," Barnes said. He pronounced it "corell," with the accent on the last syllable.

Rhodes looked over to the barn. The corner posts were stacked in under the overhang, and Barnes's pickup was there too. Bags of cement mix were also stacked inside it.

"You going to set the posts in concrete?"

"Sure enough," Barnes said. He brushed some of the hair out of his eyes with a grimy hand. "You come out here to watch me?"

"No, I came out here to talk to you."

"Talk, then. I got work to do."

Barnes had never stayed in jail more than a night, but he clearly didn't have any affection to waste on Rhodes. "I want to ask you about Dr. Martin," Rhodes said.

"That sumbitch," Barnes said. He spit a yellowish gob in the dirt he had augered up by his feet. Apparently he didn't have any affection to waste on his landlord, either.

"You and he have problems?" Rhodes asked.

"Like I told him, he comes out here botherin' me again, they're gonna have to take us both to the hospital."

"Both?"

"Yeah. They're gonna have to take *my* foot outa *his* ass." Barnes spit again.

"You tell him that yesterday?"

Barnes leaned on the auger and looked casually around. "Who says I seen him yesterday?"

"His wife," Rhodes said.

"She with him when I seen him?"

"No, she just told me that he was going to drop by for a visit."

Barnes laughed. It was an ugly sound that rattled through the phlegm in his throat. "Visit? That sumbitch don't visit. He comes around all high and mighty and tells you what you're gonna do. That's what he does."

"So what did he tell you you were going to do?" Rhodes asked.

32

"Pay up," Barnes said. "Like I wouldn't of paid up. Damn. Look around here. I've fixed up the fence, I've started in on buildin' me a corral, and he thinks I won't pay up."

"So will you?"

"Damn right, I will. Soon as I get a little cash, I'll pay. And he knows it. He just wants an excuse to run me off. I'll improve the property, then he'll get rid of me and go up two or three times on the rent to the next sucker that comes along. Well, that won't work with me. 'Course, when he saw that I was fixin' to build this corral, he didn't say too much about no rent bein' due. He'll be real glad to get it built, no cost to him. Soon as it's built, though, then he'll be bitchin' for his money again."

"So you did see him yesterday," Rhodes said.

"Maybe," Barnes said. "Maybe not."

Rhodes looked across to the other side of the road. "You lease that land over there, too?"

"Few acres," Barnes said. "Why?"

Rhodes had his eye on a small stock tank, its water lying still and flat as dark metal. There was a wooden dock built out into the tank about twenty feet. "Just wondering if there were any fish in that tank."

"Sure enough," Barnes said. "Bass and cats. I built that dock myself. Another free improvement. You like to fish?"

"Yes," Rhodes said. "Don't get much chance, though."

"Well, come ahead," Barnes said in a surprisingly generous way. Then he added, "The Doc stocked the tank. Says they're his fish. But he wouldn't mind you fishing there, probably."

"I might take him up on it, when I find him," Rhodes said.

"Don't wait on him," Barnes said. "I lease this land. I got a right to say who fishes and who don't." He paused. "What you mean, 'when you find him'?"

"He seems not to have come home yesterday," Rhodes said.

"I don't know nothin' about that," Barnes said. "Now that you mention it, I don't believe I've seen him in a week or two."

Rhodes looked at the huge man. In the fat face the mouth was set in a hard line.

Rhodes turned back to his car. "You drink the water from that well?" He walked up under the well house roof and saw that there was a heavy circular iron cover, hinged in the middle, on top of the well.

"Naw," Barnes said. "Too many minerals in it. You drink that water, you'd be stickin' to magnets. We used a little of it to water the garden one year."

Rhodes could see the garden spot off to the side of the well house. Barnes hadn't tried for a winter garden this year.

"If Dr. Martin doesn't turn up, I'll probably be seeing you again in a day or so," Rhodes said as he got into his car.

Barnes didn't answer; instead he fired up his auger.

Rhodes drove back over the cattle guard and headed back to Clearview. He wanted to have a longer talk with Mrs. Martin, find out the names of any friends who might know something about her husband, begin to question her about any little irregularities in his life of late. Then he'd go back to the jail and put out a bulletin on the Suburban. The vanity plate ought to make it easy to spot if it turned up anywhere in the state.

He was almost back in town when Hack got him on the radio to tell him that the Suburban had been found parked behind the old Milsby school.

Milsby had been a town once, but it wasn't anymore. The school was used for community functions, and Rhodes had fond memories of it because it had been at a candidates' forum there that he had met Ivy Daniel. She had been running for Justice of the Peace, and even though she hadn't won they had become better and better acquainted in the days that followed.

Rhodes drove up behind the school and saw the big Chevrolet parked there by the old fire escape just as if it had been parked for a few minutes while the owner went inside.

Standing by the Suburban were a man and two boys. The man was young, probably under thirty, and he was wearing his Sunday suit, probably bought on sale at J.C. Penney's.

The suit was black and with it he was wearing a white shirt and a dark gray tie. The two boys were dressed in slacks and sport shirts. They looked to be about six and eight years old.

Rhodes parked and walked over to the man, who stuck out his hand. "Hidy, Sheriff. My name's Clyde Cook, and these are my boys, Ed and Tim."

Rhodes shook hands with Cook. He looked at the boys, who stuck out their hands as well. He shook with them. "Glad to meet you all," he said. "You the ones called in about this Suburban?"

"That's right," Cook said. He had shaved so close earlier that morning for church that his cheeks still looked scraped. "I'm the one who called."

"Why?" Rhodes said. He was merely curious, not suspicious.

"Wellsir, my boys was out here playing behind the school this morning early—we live right over there—" he pointed to his left, where Rhodes could see a small frame house among some trees "—and the boys like to come over here and climb on the fire escape. I tell 'em not to do it, that old thing's rusty and might fall right down and them on it, but it don't do no good. Anyway, they was over here playing around and they saw this here Chevy. Ain't nobody in this neighborhood got one like this, let me tell you, and sure not one that says 'TEETH' on the plates."

"So you got worried about it?"

"Not right then, Sheriff. Sometimes folks like to pull up here on a Saturday night, and . . . well . . . you can see that where it's parked is out of sight of the road and all. Gives some folks a little privacy, I guess you could say."

Rhodes could see what he meant.

"So every now and then somebody will stall here and have to walk out. Or maybe not be fit to drive and have to walk. Not that I approve of that sort of thing, you know what I mean, but I don't like to meddle, so I usually don't say nothing.

"But this time the car was still here when the boys and me got back from church, so I thought maybe you ought to know, maybe haul it off or get it back to its owner. It stays here too

35

long, it might be tempting to somebody who needs some wheel covers, or more.''

"Did you look inside?" Rhodes asked.

"Nosir, not me. You kids?"

The two boys, who had been solemnly staring at Rhodes throughout the conversation, shook their heads from side to side.

Rhodes crossed the few feet between them to the Suburban. He tried the front door. It was unlocked. He peered inside. The keys were in the ignition. There was nothing else inside. Rhodes let out a breath. He was glad for the boys' sake that Martin wasn't there, dead or alive and passed out.

"And you didn't see anything strange yesterday or last night?" Rhodes asked. "Nobody came to your house for help or to use the phone?"

"I didn't see a thing," Cook said. "And nobody came to the house while I was there."

"You boys see anything?" Rhodes asked.

Once again they shook their heads, but said nothing.

"Anybody come by the house, talk to you or your mama about using the phone?" Cook asked.

They shook their heads again.

"Well, I'm going to leave this Suburban here for a while," Rhodes said. "I'd appreciate it if you kind of kept an eye on it, didn't let anybody touch it. I have to ask some questions around the neighborhood, see if anybody saw anything. Then we'll get it out of the way."

"It's not in the way," Cook said. "We'll keep an eye on it, right kids?"

They nodded their heads up and down.

"Nice boys," Rhodes said.

"We try to teach 'em right from wrong," Cook said. "Give 'em a little respect for the law."

Rhodes thought of Barnes and Swan. "More than most have got," he said. "More than most."

Chapter 5

THERE WERE NO OTHER HOUSES close by with a good view of the back of the school, so Rhodes went back to the jail. He wanted to get his deputy, Ruth Grady, to fingerprint the Suburban. Ruth had actually gotten an associate's degree in law enforcement from a junior college and therefore was by far the best-qualified fingerprinter in the county.

"We'll have to send her out there later," Hack said. "She's busy right now, just answered a disturbance call over to the Sunny Dale Nursing Home."

"A disturbance call?" Rhodes wasn't sure he'd heard right. "What kind of disturbance?"

"Don't know," Hack told him. "They didn't say. Just said it was an emergency."

"I'll go over there myself," Rhodes said. "Then I'll send her out to print the Suburban. After that I'm going by to see Mrs. Martin, and then I might go over to Ivy's. If you don't have any more emergencies."

Hack looked at him. "When you and that Miz Daniel

goin' to tie the knot? Seems like to me you're puttin' her off. How long's it been since you started courtin' her heavy?''

Rhodes didn't think it was any of Hack's business, but the old man didn't mean any harm. He always had to find out everything. "It hasn't been that long. When you get to be my age, you're not in any hurry to get married again.''

Hack snorted. "Your age? You ain't nothin' but a spring chicken. You wanta look at somebody old, you take a look at me. And if that Miz Daniel liked me the way she likes you, it wouldn't take me no more than a New York minute to get her to the church.''

"Well, I . . .'' Rhodes trailed off. He didn't know exactly what he'd intended to say.

Hack looked away. "Yeah, my wife died too. It ain't easy to start over, I know. Don't mind me. I just like to stick my nose in where it don't belong.''

"That's O.K. When we set the date, you'll be the first to know.''

"You gonna let me stand up with you?'' Hack paused. Then he said, "Me and Lawton?''

"Absolutely,'' Rhodes said.

"Good. Now you better get over to Sunny Dale before they tear the place down, or whatever it is they're doin'. Boy, I hope I don't ever wind up in a place like that.''

"I don't blame you much,'' Rhodes said.

It wasn't that the Sunny Dale was such a bad place, Rhodes thought as he parked in the asphalt parking area. It was just that as far as he was concerned, no nursing home was a good place to be. There was no doubt that the ones in Blacklin County provided good care, sometimes even sensitive care. It was just that . . . well, hell. It wasn't the place at all. It was the thought of being old, old and pretty much helpless, that bothered him. Probably that was what bothered Hack, too. If Hack weren't allowed to work at the jail, he might wind up in Sunny Dale or a place a lot like it, feeling useless and helpless. And one day he would find that he had become exactly what he'd feared.

Rhodes looked over the lot and saw the other county car, the one Ruth Grady had driven. Like the one Rhodes was in,

38

it was a white Plymouth with the gold shield and black lettering on the front doors. There were not many other cars in the lot. Not many visitors came at nap time.

Sunny Dale was not a large building, but it was long. All the rooms were off two halls running straight to the left and right off the large room that formed the entrance. There was a cement porch the size of the entrance room, and it was lined with chairs. No one was in the chairs now, but in the mornings, when the sun hit the porch, nearly every chair would be taken.

Rhodes opened one of the glass doors and went in. There didn't seem to be any sign of a disturbance. A family in Sunday best, mother, father, daughter, were talking to an old white-haired woman in a tattered robe. They were all seated on a couch in the entrance room, a light, airy area with lots of glass and green plants. The couch and the other furniture were shabby from repeated use, but clean.

Rhodes walked on in to the reception desk. Two women, one black, one white, both wearing white uniforms, stood behind it.

"I understand you're having a little trouble here," Rhodes said.

"That's the truth, Sheriff," the white woman said. She was wearing a black plastic name tag pinned to her uniform. The name EARLENE was embossed on it in white letters. The other woman's tag said LINDA. "We're going to have to do something about those two."

"Which two?" Rhodes asked.

"Mr. Stuart and Miz White," Linda said. "They been nothin' but trouble since she got here, practically."

"What kind of trouble?" Rhodes asked.

"Screamin', yellin', carryin' on. That kind of trouble," Earlene said. "Keeps everybody on edge. People can't sleep, can't get their work done. We may have to put 'em out."

"Where would you put them?" Rhodes asked.

"Humph. That wouldn't be my lookout. But we can't run this place with them carryin' on all the time, I'll tell you that much."

39

"Where's Mr. Patterson?" Rhodes asked. Patterson was the owner of Sunny Dale.

"Down the hall in the men's wing with Mr. Stuart. Room one-ten," Linda said.

"What about my deputy?"

"She's down the other hall," Earlene said. "Women's wing. With that Miz White. They've got 'em pretty well calmed down now, but I don't know how long it'll last. This was the worst they've been, this today. That's why we had to call. I thought we'd have a riot on our hands, I'll tell you. It was somethin' else."

"Well, I'd better check with my deputy," Rhodes said. "Thanks for the information."

"Don't mention it, Sheriff, I hope you all can get this mess straightened out, put the fear of God in those folks. Or at least the fear of the law."

Rhodes started down the hall to his left. Almost as soon as his back was turned, he heard Earlene say to Linda, "Honey, I just got to sneak back to the storeroom for a smoke. You don't mind watchin' the desk for a minute, do you?"

"Not a bit," Linda said.

Rhodes hadn't asked for Miz White's room number, but he figured he could find it. Most of the rooms he passed had their doors open. In the first room a woman who looked almost as if she were mummified lay on her back like a doll in the big double bed. Her eyes were closed, and her mouth was open. A football game was on her TV set.

In the next room a woman sat in a wheelchair, her head lolling to one side, her white hair hanging loose.

The peculiar odor of nursing homes, completely unlike that of a hospital, a combination of musty age and urine, grew stronger as Rhodes walked farther down the hall.

Near the end of the hallway he came to the room where Ruth Grady was sitting by a bed, holding an old woman's hand. Ruth looked up as Rhodes walked in the door. "Good afternoon, Sheriff," she said. "Did Hack send you to help me out?"

Hack had not had an easy time of adjusting to the fact that

the deputy Rhodes had hired to replace Johnny Sherman was a woman. In fact, he had not quite been able to address her by her name for several weeks. She had eventually won him over, however, and now they were fast friends. She was short, stout, and a thoroughly professional law officer. Rhodes felt lucky to have her on his staff.

"He didn't send me to help," Rhodes said. "He just wasn't sure what was going on out here."

"Unrequited love," Ruth said.

The woman in the bed turned to look at them. Her yellow-ish skin was a patchwork of fine wrinkles, and she had thin, short white hair. Her scalp showed through in places. "You needn't make fun, young woman," she said in a quavery voice.

"I didn't mean to," Ruth said.

"They won't let us be together, you see," Miz White said to Rhodes. "All we want is to be together."

"I see," Rhodes said, even though he didn't see.

"Why don't we go down and talk to Mr. Patterson?" Ruth said to Rhodes. "I think he can explain, and I'm sure Miz White will be fine now. Won't you?" She gently disengaged her hand from the old woman's.

"Of course I'll be fine," Miz White said. "Mr. Stuart and I'd both be fine if they'd just let us be together."

"Well," Ruth said, "we'll just have to see what we can do."

"I know you just want to go out in the hall and talk about me," Miz White told them as they went out the door. "But I don't mind. Not if you can get something done."

"I don't quite get it," Rhodes said once they were safely out of sight of Miz White's door.

"Get it? Got it! Put it in your pocket!" Someone yelled from the room they were passing. Rhodes looked in and saw a woman sitting in front of a TV set. She didn't even look back at him.

Ruth took the interruption in stride. "It's the old story. Boy meets girl, boy loses girl. Except in this case, the boy and girl are both around ninety years old."

"I'm still not sure . . ."

41

"Mr. Patterson can explain it," Ruth said.

They walked past the desk. Linda was there, writing in a book of some kind. Earlene was still gone. Probably on her second cigarette by now, Rhodes thought.

They passed rooms where old men sat mumbling to themselves, where others sat staring blankly at the walls, others where they slept restlessly. Rhodes felt a chill at the base of his spine. He wondered if he was having a midlife crisis. Or maybe he was just afraid of getting old.

Mr. Stuart was sitting in a ladder-back chair by his bed. Mr. Patterson was standing beside him.

Like his nurses, Mr. Patterson was all in white—white jacket, white pants, white shoes. His name tag, however, had no first name on it. It said MR. PATTERSON. He was a short man, not much taller than Ruth Grady, but he was wide and solid. He was about Rhodes's age, but his brownish-blond hair had no hint of gray in it, and it had been carefully styled, almost like the hair of a TV evangelist.

Mr. Stuart looked small and shrunken in the sport coat and pants he was wearing. His wrinkled neck was at least a size too small for the collar of his shirt.

Patterson looked up when the two law officers came in. "Hello, Sheriff. Sorry to have to call you about this disturbance, but things were beginning to get out of hand. Your deputy did a good job."

Rhodes looked at Ruth. She hadn't mentioned how she had managed to quell the disturbance.

"What seems to have caused all the trouble, Mr. Patterson?" Rhodes asked.

"I'll tell you that, Sheriff," Mr. Stuart said. His voice was surprisingly strong. "They won't let me and Miz White be together."

"Now see here," Patterson said. "Don't start that up again. I just won't have it." He turned to Rhodes. "You should have been here earlier, Sheriff. All the yelling, why I've never seen the likes of it."

Ruth Grady was smiling. "Me neither, not since the sixties. Biggest protest demonstration Blacklin County's ever seen, I'd bet."

42

"I wish somebody would let me in on this," Rhodes said.

"They were in the halls, in their wheelchairs, in their walkers, just every which way," Patterson said. He touched his hair as if to reassure himself that all the hurly-burly hadn't disarranged it. "You see, at nap time, we have to separate them. Men to the men's wing, women to the women's wing. It just wouldn't be . . . right any other way, if you get my meaning. We try to run a proper place here, and Mr. Stuart and Miz White are not in agreement with our policies."

"Damn right we're not," Mr. Stuart said.

"We're not set up for couples, you see," Patterson said. "We don't have . . . uh, coeducational facilities. We're for singles only, and the people who come here know that. They're apprised of the fact well in advance. So we take only those who have never married or those whose loved ones have . . . passed on."

Rhodes had caught on. "But you didn't count on having a couple fall in love."

Patterson touched his hair again. "Uh . . . yes. I mean, no. We hadn't counted on it. Not at all."

"But it happened."

"Yes. It happened. Of course, one would expect that persons of a certain age—"

"Eighty-seven!" Mr. Stuart shouted.

"—to be more mature about these matters," Mr. Patterson said. "But Mr. Stuart and Miz White have become increasingly belligerent. And today, well, things just reached a head."

"Yelling and carrying on," Rhodes said.

"Yes, and mass confusion in the halls. You can just imagine. And someone was beating on the walls with a bedpan—"

Rhodes looked at Mr. Stuart, who was smiling.

"—and Mr. Radford tried to run me down with his wheelchair," Patterson said.

"It was pretty loud when I got here, all right," Ruth Grady said, "but I didn't see the wheelchair incident. I managed to get them calmed down with Mr. Patterson's help. And Linda

43

and Earlene pitched in. I think maybe Mr. Radford, or some-body, ran over Earlene's foot.''

Rhodes turned to Mr. Stuart. "Let me see if I've got this right," he said. "You and Miz White want to share a room?"

"You got it, Sheriff," Mr. Stuart said.

"And when it came time for you to go to your rooms . . ."

"We wouldn't go. They had to take us. And we started yelling when they got us separated." Mr. Stuart looked smug.

Mr. Patterson looked unhappy. "We don't run a place for couples, we just don't," he said. "It's not . . . right, without the benefit of marriage or anything, and if they're married, they'll have to go elsewhere, because we don't have married couples either.''

"I take it this wasn't as easy to sort out as you made it sound," Rhodes said to Ruth.

"Well, no," she said, "but at least I didn't have to use my sidearm."

"Never mind," Rhodes said. "I don't think I want to hear about it." He looked at Patterson. "So where does that leave us?"

"I'm going to call their children," Patterson said. He looked completely exasperated. "I'm going to have them put out! I can't stand any more of this. Why, we were planning to have a Christmas party next week, but there is no way we could have it with all this distraction!"

"Now wait just a minute," Mr. Stuart said.

"Or maybe I could just have you arrested," Patterson said. "How about that, Sheriff. Disturbing the peace? Inciting a riot? Would any of that apply in this case?"

"Let's step out in the hall," Rhodes said. "Ruth, you keep Mr. Stuart company."

"All right," she said. "We get along fine."

Patterson's face was red and his eyes were narrowed. "You don't want to try to talk me out of this, do you, Sheriff?" he asked when they got outside the room and shut the door.

"Sure I do," Rhodes said. "It seems to me—"

"I will *not* run a bawdy house for the elderly!" Patterson said, his voice rising alarmingly. "I will *not* provide bed-mates like some big-city procurer!"

"I think you're looking at this all wrong," Rhodes said. "Can you imagine what's going to happen if the newspapers get hold of this thing? What if one of their children calls some consumer advocate? What if one of them calls that guy in Houston, the one who closed the Chicken Ranch?"

"Marvin Zindler?" Patterson said. "My God." He put both hands to his hair.

"See? Things could be worse. Whereas now, all you have to do is let two old people who aren't going to do any harm to one another sleep in the same room."

"But what if some of the others . . . ?"

"Oh," Rhodes said. "That could be a problem, all right. But how likely do you think that possibility could really be?"

"Well . . . not *very* likely, I guess."

"That's what I'd say. Could you just give it a try? They don't really have to share a room. Maybe we could compromise. Would you give it a try?"

"I . . . I suppose so," Patterson said. "We could work something out for a week, and then go on from there."

"Sure," Rhodes said. "That ought to do it."

Mr. Stuart agreed, and Rhodes left them to iron out the details. He and Ruth left Sunny Dale, and Rhodes explained to her what he wanted her to do about Dr. Samuel Martin's Suburban.

Chapter 6

"IT'S THAT CURSE, I just know it's that curse!" Mrs. Martin was pacing in front of her Paul Bunyan Christmas tree, her arms crossed under her breasts, in the same robe she had worn the night before. She looked as if she hadn't slept at all, and maybe it was the lack of sleep that had caused her to change her opinion of the reason for her husband's disappearance.

Rhodes tried to change her mind back. "The way I remember the things that were said—" he was trying to avoid the word *curse* "—he was supposed to get sick and have all his teeth fall out, not vanish."

"It's all the same. Black magic!" Mrs. Martin's hair hadn't been attended to lately, and a few strands were popping loose like stray springs from an old couch cushion. "We'll never find him. He'll be like that ship, whatever it is. *The Flying Chinaman.*"

"*Dutchman,*" Rhodes said without thinking.

"It doesn't matter! He's gone, and we'll never find him. What am I going to do?"

Rhodes wanted to suggest a little sleep. Instead he said,

"Why don't you call your doctor, have him come over. He might be able to—"

"I don't want drugs! I want my husband!"

"Why don't we sit down," Rhodes said.

"I don't want to sit down! I want—"

"I know you want your husband," Rhodes said. "And I want to find him. But we can't talk until we both sit down and try to relax."

Mrs. Martin looked at him wild-eyed for a moment. Then she sat down on one of the couches. Rhodes sat in an over-stuffed rocking chair where he could see her.

"First," Rhodes said, "I want you to know that we've found your husband's Suburban."

Mrs. Martin's mouth opened, but she couldn't seem to speak.

Rhodes went on. "Now, on that list you gave me, there was no property listed that was even near Milsby, but that's where the Suburban was, parked behind the old schoolhouse. Did your husband own any rental property around there?"

Mrs. Martin closed her mouth and thought about it. "No," she said.

"So maybe Dr. Martin went there for some other reason, or maybe the van was driven there by someone else and left. We'll find out. But we've got to look at more possibilities than those you gave me at first. Did your husband have any enemies?" Rhodes considered adding, "Besides the people he rented to?" but he thought better of it.

Mrs. Martin answered promptly this time. "Of course not. He was a man who helped people, not someone who made enemies."

It wasn't a statement that Paul Swan or Little Barnes would have agreed with, but Rhodes let it pass. He hated to ask his next question, but it had to be asked. Rhodes was in some ways a shy man, especially considering the kinds of situations his job often led him into, and there were certain areas of a person's private life that he didn't like to pry into.

"Did your husband . . . did he ever . . . stay out late at night on other occasions?" he asked.

47

Mrs. Martin looked at him sharply. The loose springs of hair vibrated. "Just what is that supposed to mean?"

Rhodes returned her look. "It means, did he ever spend time out of the house when he wasn't on business."

"I don't understand."

Rhodes could tell he wasn't going to get any help. In fact, he almost felt that Mrs. Martin was making things deliberately difficult. "Did he like to step out without you? With other women?"

"Other women?" Mrs. Martin was clearly horrified. "Of course not! I don't see how you could even ask such a question. Listen to me, Sheriff. My husband was a fine man. A credit to this community. A member of the Lion's Club."

That cinches it, Rhodes thought. A member of the Lion's Club would never run around on his wife.

"He would never dream of looking at another woman. What I want—and I want it done at once—is for you to arrest that witch that cursed my husband and put her behind bars!"

At least she didn't mention knowing the commissioners again, Rhodes thought. He said, "We can't prove that she's done anything yet."

"You can prove that she cursed him. That should be enough."

"I'll see what can be done about it," Rhodes said, rising from the chair. It was like trying to get out of a marshmallow. "Meanwhile I'd like to ask you to do a few things for me."

"What things?"

"I'd appreciate it if you could call your husband's office staff tomorrow and ask them to stay open for business as usual. Tell them not to cancel any of the appointments. I want to go by and talk to them again."

"Well . . . all right. But I don't see why."

"You never know what might be important in cases like these," Rhodes said. He had no idea what that meant, but it seemed to satisfy Mrs. Martin.

"I see," she said. "I'll do it, then."

After Rhodes left and began his drive out to Milsby, he thought about something he'd heard somewhere, something about a lady who protested too much. It made him wonder

48

about Dr. Samuel Martin and about the good doctor's relationship with his wife.

Ruth Grady had finished with the Suburban by the time Rhodes got back to Milsby. Ed and Tim Cook, still in their sport shirts and slacks, were watching her from a respectful distance. Rhodes waved to them, and they waved back.

"Find anything?" he asked Ruth.

"Not a thing. Whoever drove this van here must have wiped it down. Probably learned that from watching television. Did a good job, too. Or maybe the owner just kept it real clean. But even at that there should be prints on the door handles and the wheel. I couldn't raise a thing."

"Did you search it?"

Ruth shook her head. "Sure did. Another blank. I vacuumed it, too, but I don't think we'll turn up much of anything there, either."

"Well, we had to try." Rhodes walked over to Ed and Tim. "You two did a fine job of watching," he said. "I think it'd be all right for you to go on home now. Thanks for the help."

The two boys looked at one another, then stuck out their hands.

Rhodes shook each hand.

Ed and Tim turned without saying a word and started walking toward their house. Rhodes watched them go. Big-time crime really gets the kids excited, he thought.

He walked back over to where Ruth Grady stood by the van. "We'll take the keys and leave this here for a while. I'll come back and get it later."

"Fine," Ruth said. "Why don't you fill me in on the whole story."

Rhodes told her about Martin, Betsy Higgins and the Curse, Phil Swan, and Little Barnes.

"She really put a curse on him?"

"Right there in his office," Rhodes said.

"I've always wanted to do that to a dentist," Ruth said.

"If you ever do," Rhodes said, "please don't do it in this county."

It was late afternoon getting on toward evening when Rhodes pulled up in front of Ivy Daniel's house. He sat in the car for a few minutes before getting out. He knew that she was expecting him to set a date for their marriage, though she'd never actually said a word about it, but somehow he couldn't bring himself to do it. And he didn't know why. He didn't like to think of himself as a coward, and he wasn't. Not about some things at least. Maybe he was, about this.

He sighed and got out of the car.

As usual Ivy seemed glad to see him, giving him a quick hug and a kiss on the cheek. And Rhodes was glad to see her. Her neat figure, her short, graying hair, the way she smiled, all those things made him feel a really deep glow of pleasure.

"Want to do some law work?" he asked.

"Sure," she said. "Who do you want me to arrest?"

"It's not quite that drastic. I just need a wheel man. Or person."

"I'm your man." She laughed. "Or person. Would you care to be more specific?"

Rhodes told her the whole story, just as he'd told it to Ruth Grady.

"Do you think he's been kidnapped?" she asked.

Rhodes had entertained several thoughts. Kidnapping hadn't been one of them. "No note," he said. "No phone calls. At first I thought he'd just gone out on a party, but now I don't know. It's pretty certain that he didn't leave that van there, all wiped down."

"Then we can say that you suspect 'foul play'?" She pretended to be writing notes on a nonexistent pad.

"I don't say things like that," Rhodes told her.

"I know. It's part of your charm."

Rhodes didn't say anything to that. He didn't know what *to* say. He didn't think of himself as having any charm, and he thought maybe Ivy was kidding him.

"How about some food?" she asked.

Rhodes tried to think of the last time he'd eaten. He couldn't remember. Maybe he wouldn't need that stationary bike after all. He sneaked a look at his stomach. Was it any smaller? He couldn't tell. "What do you have?" he asked.

"I cooked a roast today. We could warm it up. I've got mashed potatoes, carrots, and English peas. I think I may even have some Dr Pepper in the refrigerator."

"I'll just have water," Rhodes said. "But the rest sounds great. Then we can go get the van."

"I'll warm it up," Ivy said. "It won't take long."

It didn't. The food was delicious and didn't have the "warmed-up" taste that Rhodes always managed to achieve when he had leftovers. When he finished, his belt felt much tighter than it had felt earlier. Well, there was always the bike.

On the way to Milsby Rhodes turned on the radio to the local FM station, just as the disc jockey was announcing that he would play a number called "We Don't Have to Take Our Clothes Off to Have a Good Time."

"This one was a real biggie only a few months back," the dj said in his excited voice.

Rhodes thought that he probably hadn't heard the title correctly, or that the dj was making some kind of joke. Then the song began. There was no joke.

"Whatever happened to songs like 'Be-Bop Baby'?" he asked.

"I don't know," Ivy said. "Do you think he's right?"

"Who?" Rhodes asked.

"The man singing that song."

"I . . . uh . . . I . . ."

Ivy laughed aloud. "Never mind," she said.

Rhodes turned off the radio. "Uh, I might get a call from Hack. Need to be able to hear it."

Ivy didn't say anything, though Rhodes was pretty sure he heard her chuckle. When he looked over at her, her face was composed, the dim lights of the dash giving nothing away. He changed the subject by telling her more about Mrs. Martin.

"And you think she really believes that the curse had something to do with her husband's disappearance?" Ivy asked.

"I don't think so, not really. I think she's just tired. She probably hasn't slept in thirty-six hours. Maybe she'll be able to think better if she can get some rest."

"But she wouldn't let you send for a doctor."

"No, but I think she'll sleep without help if she just lets her guard down for a few minutes. There was something funny about the way she acted, though. Something that didn't have anything to do with the lack of sleep."

"How do you mean?"

Rhodes told her about the 'protesting too much' business.

"*Hamlet*," Ivy said. "That's from *Hamlet*. Hamlet says it about his mother, that she protests too much."

Rhodes tried to remember if he'd ever read *Hamlet*. Probably not. "Must be something I picked up from Kathy," he said.

"So you think maybe his wife had something to do with his disappearance?"

"I don't know what I think right now. I can't see any reason why she would have. But maybe I ought to talk to their insurance agent tomorrow."

"You completely discount the curse?"

"Now don't tell me that you believe in curses."

"You never know," Ivy said. "Some women have strange powers."

Rhodes looked at her again. He still couldn't tell whether she was kidding.

Ivy followed the county car back to the jail. They parked the van in the rear of the old structure and Rhodes took the keys inside. Ivy went in with him.

"Hello, Hack," she said.

Hack got out of his chair by the radio. He always got up when Ivy visited the jail. " 'Evenin', Miz Daniel," he said.

"Keep your seat, Hack," Rhodes said. "We won't be staying. Any new customers?"

"Nope," Hack said. "But it won't be long. Closer it gets to Christmas, the more customers we'll get. Just like every year."

"Why is that?" Ivy asked.

52

Hack shook his head. He hadn't sat back down. "People who can't afford presents. They'll rob somebody or steal somethin'. Have to spend Christmas in the jailhouse. Makes it sad for the whole family."

Ivy looked around the room, at the gunrack, the flyers on various desperate criminals, the untidy desks. "You don't have a Christmas tree," she said. Rhodes could sense the accusation in her tone.

"We never have had one," Hack said. "It might not be a bad idea, though."

"Where do you spend Christmas, Hack? You and Lawton?" Ivy asked.

"Right here," Hack said. "Sheriff usually comes in and we have a sandwich or somethin'."

Rhodes felt an obscure need to defend himself. "Now you know that we had turkey and dressing last year, Hack."

"Yeah, that's right. Miz Stutts sent over too much, so we got the extra."

Miz Stutts was the woman who had a contract to feed the prisoners. She did such a good job that Rhodes would not have been surprised if some of the Christmas Day prisoners hadn't gotten themselves jailed on purpose.

"It was good anyway," Rhodes said.

"Sure was," Hack said. "I hope she sends too much this year. Sure would beat them sandwiches we usually get."

"I'm going to bring in a Christmas tree," Ivy said. "And I'll fix the Christmas dinner."

Rhodes opened his mouth to protest, but nothing came out.

"That sounds mighty nice," Hack said. "You sure you want to do that?"

"Of course I'm sure. Everybody deserves a Christmas dinner. And everybody ought to have a Christmas tree, too."

"I guess so," Hack said. "What do you think, Sheriff?"

"Sounds fine to me, too," Rhodes said.

"Then that's settled," Ivy said. "I think there's plenty of room for a tree in here."

"Long as it don't have those needles that drop off on the floor," Lawton said, coming in from the cellblock area. "I

53

purely do hate to have to sweep up those needles. I remember once we had one of those trees at home, and those needles got in the vacuum cleaner and like to have burned up the motor before we figured out what was stuck in there.''

"We can cut a cedar tree," Ivy said. "There's plenty of them around here. And they don't have needles."

"Good," Lawton said. Then he looked at Rhodes. "Uh, Sheriff, I was wonderin' if I could have a word with you."

"Sure," Rhodes said, wondering what was up. He followed Lawton out the door and up the stairs to the cells on the second floor.

"Is there something wrong with the cells?" Rhodes asked.

"Naw, nothin' like that," Lawton said. "It's just that me and Hack've been talkin' about this here curse business."

"So?"

"So we been thinkin' maybe there's somethin' to it. I mean, not really, but like in the case of the mind influencin' the body. You know what I mean?"

"Not exactly," Rhodes said. "Maybe you better tell me."

"It's like that voodoo stuff," Lawton said. The cell area was not very well lighted, but Rhodes could see well enough to be able to tell that Lawton was absolutely serious.

"Voodoo?" he said.

"Yeah, like when somebody puts a curse on you or sticks pins in them voodoo dolls and you die, or at least get sick because you know you're supposed to. The mind influences the body."

"Like the guy that died of the rattlesnake bite," Rhodes said.

"Right!" Lawton said. They both remembered the story well because the host of a TV wildlife program had told it so often. Both Lawton and Rhodes had been faithful viewers of the show. "Everybody told him to watch out for snakes, so he was out one day and backed into that whatchamacall-it—"

"We always called it a Devil's Claw," Rhodes said.

"—that Devil's Claw. And when the two points of that thing stuck him, the seeds in the pod rattled together and sounded to him like a snake. The poor sucker died before they could get him to a hospital because he thought he'd been snake bit.''

"But Dr. Martin's teeth didn't fall out," Rhodes said. "He disappeared."

"Same thing," Lawton said.

First Mrs. Martin, now Lawton and Hack. "Where do you think his mind influenced him to go?" Rhodes asked.

"How should I know?" Lawton said. "You're the sheriff, not me."

"O.K.," Rhodes told him. "I'll think about it."

"Good," Lawton said. "You can go on back down now. I got to work on one of the bunks up here. Leg needs straightenin'."

Rhodes went back downstairs, and he and Ivy left. As they walked to the car she asked, "What did Lawton want?"

"Well, you might say he was giving me his theory of the Martin disappearance."

"Which is?"

"A case of the mind influencing the body."

"I don't think—"

"Like voodoo."

"Oh."

"So what were you and Hack discussing while I was gone? Decorations for the tree?"

"Not exactly. He was telling me that he'd seen where a famous scientist had discovered Atlantis."

First voodoo, now Atlantis, Rhodes thought. "Where did he see that?" he asked.

"In one of those tabloids. He read the front page while he was in the check-out line at Wal-Mart."

"I knew he was getting too much time off," Rhodes said. "He and Lawton together will believe just about anything."

"And of course you don't hold with curses at all."

"Not much," Rhodes said.

He didn't change his mind, even though Mrs. Martin was murdered that night.

Chapter 7

RHODES WAS THE ONE who found her.

He called twice to remind her about letting the office staff know to keep the office open all day, but he got no answer. Then he called the office staff, who hadn't heard either. So Rhodes asked them himself to stay open even though the doctor didn't show up and to cancel the appointments only when the patients arrived. Then he drove to the Martins' house.

He knocked and rang the bell.

No answer. Thinking that maybe Mrs. Martin had taken a sleeping pill, he started walking around the house. He got only as far as the garage, where he noticed that the door leading into the house was ajar.

He walked past the cars and opened the door, calling Mrs. Martin's name. Still no answer.

He went into the house, continuing to call out. He was in the kitchen, a kitchen such as he had never seen before, filled with every imaginable gadget—under-the-cabinet coffee maker and can opener, microwave, trash compactor, refrigerator that would give you ice cubes in a glass through an opening in the door, food processor, juicer, blender, and several things Rhodes couldn't even put a name to.

But no sign of Mrs. Martin.

She wasn't far, however. Rhodes found her in the next room, right beside the couch where she had sat the previous day to talk to him. She was still wearing the same robe. The main difference was that her still stiff hair was stained a dark black by blood.

Rhodes looked around the room. The place looked as if it had been systematically searched. The desk drawers were open, and papers had been spilled on the floor. The presents under the tree had been opened, too, though the contents of the boxes—sweaters, shirts, slacks—had apparently been left there. The books had been removed from the shelving and were lying on the floor. The VCR was missing from the home entertainment center, along with the TV set.

Rhodes knew he had to make the necessary phone calls, but he wanted to look at the rest of the house first. He walked carefully around Mrs. Martin's body and through the room, then down a hall leading to the rest of the house.

Each room seemed to have been searched in the same way as the first. Closets were open, clothing scattered about. Shelves had been ransacked. Pictures had been taken off the walls. Rhodes was not able to determine what might be missing from the rooms, not having looked in them before.

He went back to Mrs. Martin's body. Kneeling down beside it, he looked at the spot of blood on her head. She had been hit with something, but whatever it was had not been left behind. Her robe was not so tightly belted as it had been, but there were no other signs of a struggle.

He touched the body. It was quite cold. Mrs. Martin had been dead for a while.

Rhodes thought things through for a minute, then got up and went to the yellow telephone hanging from one of the kitchen cabinets to make his calls.

Clyde Ballinger came out with the ambulance that would be taking the body to Ballinger's Funeral Home. He and Rhodes stood in the kitchen while the Justice of the Peace

57

pronounced Mrs. Martin dead, a job that did not require much expertise in this instance. "Did you call Dr. White about an autopsy on this one?" Ballinger asked. He had a loud, almost braying, voice, though when he was performing as a funeral director it could be as smooth and soothing as anyone's. At those times he reminded Rhodes of a short, fat Vincent Price. Not now, however. His voice could have been heard next door. He was not in awe of death.

"Yes," Rhodes said. "He'll meet you there."

"Hell, you don't need him to tell you the cause of death," Ballinger said. "Of course I know you'll want him to look for clues. Skin under the fingernails, that sort of thing."

Ballinger liked to sit in his office behind the funeral home and read crime fiction. He thought he knew as much about crime solving as anyone, and it sometimes seemed to Rhodes as if he thought he knew more than the law-enforcement officials in Blacklin County.

"Of course she might have been raped," Ballinger said. "In that case the killer would have had to take her robe off and put it back on her. Or at least disarrange it and rearrange it. Might be some prints on that robe. I remember a case in the 87th Precinct—"

"Cloth doesn't take prints very well," Rhodes said. He didn't want Ballinger to get started about the 87th Precinct. He followed the adventures of Carella and Hawes religiously and could quote at length from their cases.

"That shiny kind of cloth might," Ballinger said. "You ought to try at least."

"I'll think about it," Rhodes said.

"It's a good idea," Ballinger insisted.

"I know," Rhodes said. "I'll see to it."

After the body was removed and the J.P. had left, Ballinger went back to the funeral home and Rhodes went outside. He was walking around outside when he saw someone going into the garage.

"Who's there?" he called.

"It's just me," a quavery voice answered. "Is that you, Sheriff?"

Rhodes walked around to the garage. Standing beside the

58

'57 Chevy was a small, very old woman, about the same age as Mr. Stuart, Rhodes thought. Although the weather was still unseasonably warm, she was wearing a long black cloth coat and had a red shawl wrapped around her shoulders. A maroon scarf was tied around her head. She peered at Rhodes over the top of a pair of half-glasses that she had probably bought at the drugstore.

"Good morning," Rhodes said. "What can I do for you?"

"I can do somethin' for you," she said. "That is, I can if there's been some monkey business goin' on over here." Her voice was thin and breathy, but no longer quavery.

"There has," Rhodes said. "Been some monkey business, I mean."

"I thought so," the old woman said. "I thought I saw somebody lurkin' around here last night."

"You might be able to help me then, Miz . . ."

"West. Maddy West."

"What did you see last night, Miz West?"

"I was out for my walk," she said. "I go out every evenin' for a walk. When you get to be my age, you need to keep the blood movin' around, so I go for a walk. I usually walk by here, and I did last night. I live just down the street and around the corner and over a block or two."

Rhodes hadn't thought she lived in this neighborhood.

She seemed to read his thoughts. "I don't have the money to live in a house like this one," she said. "But I like to walk by and look at them. Don't hurt nothin'. Anyway, when I saw that ambulance—" she pronounced it with the accent on "lance" "—I knew that there was some trouble, and I thought to myself that I'd just take my walk early today. So here I am."

"Here you are," Rhodes said. "You were going to tell me what you could do for me."

"So I was. I do tend to be a little forgetful now and then these days. I talk too much, too. You might have noticed that. And when you talk too much, you don't get much said, if you take my meaning."

"I think I do," Rhodes said.

"Yeah, you look like a smart young man." Miz West took

59

off her glasses and rubbed at them with the ends of her scarf. "What was it that I was talkin' about?"

"How you could help me," Rhodes said.

"Oh. Well, I saw somethin' that looked funny to me, like what you don't see around here much. You see a lot of things like this." She pointed to the Chevy. "Or that." She pointed to the Lincoln. "But not like what I saw."

"And what was that?" Rhodes asked.

"A pickup," Miz West said. "Now you see some fancy pickups around here, but this wasn't a fancy one."

"There must have been something funny about it to make you notice it, then," Rhodes said. "Even if it wasn't fancy."

"There sure was," Miz West said, settling her glasses on her nose. "It had one of them little yellow signs hanging in the back window. One thing you can bet on, and that's the truth. Even if someone around here would have a pickup like that, there ain't a single one of 'em would put one of them signs in the back window."

That was true enough, Rhodes thought. "Do you remember what the sign said?"

"Nope. Can't see too well without my glasses. But it was there, all right, hanging in that little back window. You can bet on that."

Rhodes believed her, though he would have been happier if she had been able to read the sign. He couldn't help wondering if it said BULLRIDER ON BOARD.

Things were hectic at the dental parlor of Dr. Samuel Martin, whereabouts unknown. Rhodes walked in on an angry patient, a middle-aged woman who was irate that Dr. Martin was not in. "My time is as valuable as his," the woman said. "I have a good mind to see a lawyer and send Dr. Martin a bill. That's what he'd do if *I* failed to show up for an appointment!"

"I'm sure we can reschedule—" Tammy Green said.

The woman drew herself up huffily, which wasn't easy since she was only about five feet three. "I have no desire to reschedule. And please don't send me any reminders. I don't

believe I'll be needing the services of Dr. Martin again."
She turned to go and saw Rhodes.

"Dr. Martin is involved in a little police matter," Rhodes said. "He's not missing today because he wants to."

The woman was flustered. "I . . . well, of course if it's a police matter. . . ." Then she had a new thought. "Has he been arrested? So many of these doctors and dentists today . . ."

"No," Rhodes said. "He hasn't been arrested." Looking at the woman's doughy face, hungry for some tidbit of scandal, he was tempted to make her day by telling her about the curse, the disappearance, and Mrs. Martin's death. But of course he couldn't do that. "As far as we know right now, he's in no trouble at all." Rhodes didn't add that it was what he *didn't* know that bothered him.

"Well . . ." the woman said. "I suppose . . ." She turned back to Tammy. "You may reschedule me. But please make it for a morning hour."

"I'll do that," Tammy said. "And shall I send you a reminder?"

The woman looked surprised. "Of course," she said.

When the woman left, Rhodes stepped up to the window behind which Tammy sat in a beige secretarial chair on wheels. A clipboard for the patients to sign hung on a nail beside the window, and Rhodes glanced at it. Most of the appointment times had names signed beside them with the ballpoint pen that was tied to the clipboard with a piece of white string.

"Had many like her today?" he asked. Assuming that she had been the last to sign in, her name was Sally Brandon.

"Not too many," Tammy said. "Most of our patients are very understanding in an emergency."

"Had any who didn't show up?"

"Only Mrs. Robinson, and she called. She's got the shingles."

"That about usual?"

"What do you mean?"

"I mean, about usual for no-shows," Rhodes said.

"Oh. Yes, I guess it is."

61

Rhodes nodded. It would have been a very long shot indeed had one of Martin's Monday patients been somehow involved with his disappearance and thus known that there was no need to keep the appointment.

"Sheriff?" Tammy said.

"What?" Rhodes said.

"Could you maybe tell us what this is all about? I mean, we haven't had too much trouble, but rescheduling the appointments isn't easy, and we haven't heard from Dr. Martin. When you called . . ."

When he had called, Rhodes hadn't told the office staff anything. He had implied that perhaps the reason for his wanting them to open without their boss had something to do with Betsy Higgins and her curse, but he hadn't been too specific. Now, he realized, he was going to have to be very specific. And besides that, he was going to have to give them the even worse news about Mrs. Martin.

"Is there some way you could close up now?" Rhodes asked. "Put a funeral wreath on the door or something?" It wouldn't be too much of a deception; soon enough it would be literally true.

"I . . . I guess so," Tammy said. "If you're sure it's all right. We do have a wreath, and a sign saying that all appointments have been rescheduled."

"That ought to do the trick," Rhodes said.

After Tammy put the wreath on the door, she and Rhodes went on back to the kitchen. Carol Shamblin and Jamie Fox met them there. Rhodes, not enjoying the job, told them about Dr. Martin. Then, liking it even less, he told them about Mrs. Martin.

Tammy cried quietly. Carol went over and looked silently out the window at the pecan tree, and Jamie sat at the table. "Do you know who did it?" Jamie asked.

"To tell the truth," Rhodes said, "no." He looked at Carol's back, the rigid spine showing tight against the cloth of her white uniform.

"And Dr. Martin?" Tammy said. "What about him? Where could he be?"

"I don't know that, either," Rhodes said.

"What should we do?" Tammy asked. "I mean, I guess Carol could do some of the cleaning, like she did when she got here today, but what about . . . everything else?"

Rhodes didn't know exactly what to say. He wasn't used to giving advice about how to conduct business, particularly in dentists' offices. "I think you'd better start calling your patients and asking them to find another dentist," he said, realizing for the first time that he really never expected to see Dr. Martin again. Not alive.

Tammy started crying again. Jamie joined her. Rhodes walked back out into the reception area, waited a few minutes, then went back to the kitchen. Everyone seemed fairly composed now, though Carol was still staring through the window.

"I'm going to do all I can," he said. It was lame, he knew, but there was really nothing else he could say.

"We know you are, Sheriff," Tammy said. "I just hope you get whoever did it, so they'll get what they deserve."

"I'll try," Rhodes said. That much he could promise.

The south wind, unduly warm and humid, was sending the dead leaves scraping across the parking lot behind Ballinger's Funeral Home. Rhodes parked his car and got out, heading for Ballinger's office.

Just as he had almost reached the door someone called his name. He turned to see Dr. White coming out the back door of the funeral home, followed closely by Clyde Ballinger. White was the one who had called out.

"I was hoping to catch you," Rhodes said. "You have anything to tell me?"

"Not much," Dr. White said. "She obviously hadn't eaten anything for quite a while, and so it's hard to fix the time of death."

"I think we can guess at that pretty well," Rhodes said. "It was last night sometime, no doubt about it."

"Well, that's not very close," Dr. White said. "Anyway, she was killed by a blow to the head, as you probably guessed. Caved in the left temple. I'd say it was something like a

63

crowbar, just guessing. Something long and thin, anyway. No sign of a struggle, though. Not at all.''

"That's it?" Rhodes asked.

"That's it," White said. "Sorry."

"Not your fault," Rhodes said. "Thanks."

"Call me if you need anything else," White said. He was a retired doctor who did the county's autopsies if they weren't too complicated. They usually weren't.

"I'll do that," Rhodes said as White walked over to a three-year-old Pontiac and got in.

"What a story this one would make," Ballinger said as the Pontiac drove out of the parking lot. "Wealthy dentist's wife murdered in her dressing gown, house ransacked. Course you'd have to throw in a little sex if you wanted it to sell. They knew how to handle that stuff in the old days. You ever read anything by Jonathan Craig?"

Rhodes had to admit that he hadn't. Most of Ballinger's enthusiasms were writers Rhodes had never heard of.

"He wrote stuff sort of like the 87th Precinct books," Ballinger said. "Only not exactly. Police stuff, though. They always had this kinky sex angle, but since they were written in the fifties he had to play it down and build it up at the same time. You know."

Rhodes didn't know, but he nodded.

"This could be the same way. I bet old Pete Selby—"

"Who's he?" Rhodes asked.

"The main cop in the books. Anyway, I bet he—"

"I bet he would, too," Rhodes said. "But he's not here, and this isn't the fifties. You wouldn't hint to anyone that there was a sex angle to this would you, Clyde?"

Ballinger's round face took on a look of injured innocence. "You know me better than that, Sheriff."

It was true. Rhodes knew him better than that. He was letting his own frustrations show. "Sorry," he said. "It's just that these things don't always work out like they do in stories."

"Yeah," Ballinger said. "I know." He looked at the asphalt of the parking lot for a second or two. "Say, what about Dr. Martin? How does he figure in this?"

Rhodes told him. "I know you won't breathe a word of this," he said.

"Of course not," Ballinger said. "Boy, this is even better than I thought. Husband missing, wife murdered . . ."

"It's not as much fun as it sounds like," Rhodes said.

"I guess you're right. I'm glad I don't have your job. I'd rather read about it."

Rhodes didn't say that he was glad he didn't have Ballinger's job. He didn't want to hurt his feelings again.

Chapter 8

RHODES DROVE AIMLESSLY after leaving the funeral home. He was trying to put the pieces together in his mind. Missing husband, murdered wife. Abandoned vehicle. Bad blood between the missing husband and his renters, particularly Betsy Higgins and her friend Phil Swan. And Little Barnes. Mrs. Martin's protesting too much. Looked like he'd *never* find out what that meant now. The pickup Miz West had seen, the one with a yellow diamond in the back window. But no idea of what was on the diamond. Well, an idea, all right, but nothing that was anywhere near certain.

This was the way Rhodes always worked, nothing scientific about it. He often thought that it might be interesting to live in a big city, work on a force with computers and labs, encounter all sorts of strange and unusual crimes. But he knew that he wouldn't be happy there. His method was to ask questions, probe into things, and rely on his instincts. So far he had been reasonably successful, given the kind of crime he had to deal with in Blacklin County. But this was beginning to look too complicated. He would give it a try, though, and go with what he had to work with. Maybe things would turn out to be simpler than they looked, though they seldom did.

He supposed that it was time to pay a visit to Betsy Higgins and Phil Swan again. So far theirs was the only pickup, at least the only one with a diamond in the window, that had turned up in the case.

He looked around to see where he was, having been driving more or less on automatic pilot. He had gotten a little way out of town, out in the area by the new high school. He looked at the windowless building and wondered what it would be like to attend classes in it, walking the coolly lit fluorescent halls, never seeing the daylight until you got out of class in the afternoon. Maybe it wasn't so bad, and he was sure the air conditioning was more efficient in a building like that. Still, it wasn't a place where he'd want to spend every day.

He turned the car around and looked over at the football stadium. It was the same stadium that had once stood on the opposite side of town, the same one that had been the stadium ever since Rhodes could remember. It had simply been disassembled and moved, then put back together. At least some things stayed the same.

Rhodes called Hack on the radio to tell him where he'd be.

"You sure you don't want some back-up, Sheriff?" Hack asked.

Rhodes didn't like to go into these things on the radio. "I'm only going over there to ask a few questions," he said.

"Yeah," Hack said. "That's what you thought about that Rapper that time."

Rhodes made a face. Rapper and his buddy Jase had made him look bad, all right. "I'll be fine," he said.

"Yeah," Hack said. "You gonna call and check in anytime soon?"

"Between thirty minutes and an hour," Rhodes told him.

"I'm countin' on it," Hack said.

Rhodes hoped that Phil Swan didn't have a scanner. He hadn't seen one when he'd looked the house over, but he'd been in only the one room. It was possible that the scanner was in the bedroom with the TV set. If it was, there wouldn't be anyone at home when he got there.

He drove up to the house and parked. The pickup was there, so that probably meant no scanner, or at least not one that was turned on. Or maybe there was a scanner, it was turned on, Swan and Higgins knew he was coming, and they just didn't care because they were completely innocent of anything wrong. Life certainly got complicated at times.

Rhodes knocked at the door.

No answer.

He knocked again, harder.

Still no answer.

He couldn't force his way in, but he tried the doorknob just in case the door was not locked.

It was. He turned the knob as hard as he could, but the door wouldn't budge.

If the truck was there, Rhodes thought, someone must be in the house. He pounded on the door facing with the heel of his hand, so hard that he thought the neighbors might hear. But no one in the nearby houses put a head out a window, and there was no sound from inside the one he was interested in.

Then he heard something, something that sounded like the door of a pickup being opened as quietly as possible. There was no covering up the sound of the door latch releasing, however.

Rhodes stepped off the porch and started around to the side of the house. He saw Betsy Higgins getting into the pickup. Phil Swan was walking around to the driver's side.

"Just a minute," Rhodes said. "I'd like to talk to you two."

Betsy Higgins slammed the door on her side. Swan turned to face Rhodes. "We got nothing to say to you," he said.

"Maybe not," Rhodes said, "but I have to ask a couple of questions."

"You just back off," Swan said, "and you won't get hurt. I'm going to get in this truck and drive away, and we won't be bothering you again."

"Maybe you can drive off later," Rhodes said. "After

I've asked you the questions.'' Swan looked even bigger than he remembered. Rhodes's pipsqueak neck tingled in anticipation of Swan's fingers encircling it.

Suddenly Swan seemed to give in. ''All right, ask. But don't take too long.''

Rhodes would have liked to ask why Swan was in such a hurry, but he decided to start with what he'd come for. ''I'd like to know where you were last night, early. About six or six-thirty.''

Swan looked over his shoulder to where Betsy Higgins sat in the pickup. Her head barely showed through the back window beside the sign that said BULLRIDER ON BOARD. Then Swan looked back at Rhodes, but his eyes were shifty. ''I was right here,'' he said.

''Right out here in the yard?''

''Don't start tryin' to trip me up, Sheriff,'' Swan said, his bass voice rumbling. ''You know what I mean.''

''No,'' Rhodes said. ''I don't.''

''I mean I was right here at the house. Probably watching the news on TV. Or maybe *Wheel of Fortune*. That comes on right after the news, don't it?''

''I don't know,'' Rhodes said. He didn't. He never watched game shows, just old movies.

''Well, it does. I watch it ever' night.''

Rhodes didn't believe him. ''I'll just ask Miz Higgins the same thing,'' he said, stepping toward the pickup.

Swan stepped in front of him. ''You can take my word for it,'' he said.

''I wish I could,'' Rhodes said. ''But I have to double check.'' He took another step.

Swan reached out a hand the size of a Virginia ham and put it against Rhodes's chest. ''No, you don't.''

Rhodes tried to step around him, but Swan was quick as well as big. He pushed at Rhodes again, this time shoving him back a good five feet.

''I wish you wouldn't do that,'' Rhodes said. He also wished he'd asked Hack for some backup. It was funny how a simple little thing like asking questions could get some people so riled up. "You know I have to talk to Miz Higgins," he said.

"You've done all the talkin' you're goin' to do," Swan said. He lowered his head and charged at Rhodes.

Rhodes wasn't too surprised. He tried to sidestep the charge, with the idea of swinging his fists and hitting Swan in the kidneys as he passed, but it didn't work.

Swan was too quick. He saw or sensed Rhodes's movement and turned to counter it, opening his arms wide as if to grab Rhodes and squeeze him.

Rhodes tried to bring his clasped fists up and hit Swan's arms, while at the same time backing away from him.

That didn't work either. Rhodes caught his heel on a tuft of grass or dirt and fell down, landing hard on his coccyx.

Swan reached for him, and Rhodes swung his fists, scooting along the ground on his butt while pushing with his heels. So far it was the most undignified fight he'd ever been in. He'd managed to hit Swan's arms, but that hadn't even slowed the big man down.

Rhodes felt the side of the house at his back and knew he was stopped. He gathered his feet and launched himself at Swan's legs.

It was like hitting a couple of tree stumps, but at least Swan was surprised. He staggered backward, and Rhodes tightened his grip around his knees, trying to press the legs together.

Swan windmilled his arms, beginning to lose his balance. Rhodes held on, and Swan crashed to the ground like a bulldogged steer. He was arching his back and digging his heels into the dirt, trying to break Rhodes's hold and throw him off.

It was all Rhodes could do to keep his grip. He would have liked to maneuver upward, perhaps getting a hold around Swan's arms, but it was impossible. Rhodes's hands were getting scraped against the ground, and he could feel the skin peeling off their backs.

Swan was filling the air with profanity and an imaginative array of vulgar colloquialisms, all the while twisting and turning like a dervish. Suddenly he stopped. He tried to sit

70

up, and when that didn't succeed he began banging on Rhodes's head with fists as hard as the rubber mallets body men used to beat the dents out of car fenders.

Through the ringing is his ears Rhodes heard the pickup start. Betsy Higgins wasn't going to wait around for her boyfriend any longer. No wonder Swan was getting desperate. Rhodes figured that if he could just hold on a little longer she would be gone. Then maybe Swan would listen to reason.

But he couldn't hold on. With one last mighty effort Swan heaved, hit, and kicked at the same time. Rhodes lost his grip and went rolling across the grass.

When he looked up, Swan was getting to his feet and the pickup was rolling.

It was rolling right at Rhodes.

Betsy Higgins seemed to have decided that Rhodes should be punished for beating on her boyfriend, and apparently she was going to punish him by running him down with the truck.

Rhodes saw the tires chewing dirt, and he threw himself to one side, breaking his fall with his hands. He felt his palms burn, and he knew that he had now scraped all the skin off both sides of his hands.

But at least Betsy Higgins had missed him.

She was not discouraged, however. Rhodes heard the gears grind as she shifted into reverse, and then the tailgate of the pickup was speeding toward him.

Since he hadn't gotten up, he at least didn't have to fall again. Instead he rolled as fast as he could to the side.

Betsy, unable to see him in the mirror, roared past him and clipped Phil Swan with the fender as he desperately tried to avoid her. Rhodes heard him groan as he fell to the side.

Betsy Higgins didn't see him fall. She was concentrating on Rhodes, and she shifted into low, gunning the engine and popping the clutch before getting the gears completely engaged. The pickup leaped forward and died. Betsy ground the starter, and Rhodes could smell gasoline fumes. She had flooded the engine.

Rhodes got to his feet, trying not to groan, and headed for the driver's door. He had almost made it when Phil Swan appeared from around the back of the truck, hanging on to the side. Seeing Rhodes, he let go of his support and launched himself at the sheriff.

Swan was not nearly as quick as he had been, but Rhodes was in no condition to attempt tricky evasive measures. Swan rammed into him and they both stumbled backward, striking the ground with Swan on top. The impact forced most of the breath out of Rhodes's lungs, and he gasped for air.

Swan took advantage of the situation to begin pounding on Rhodes's face and chest, but Rhodes was able to get a pretty good swing at Swan's hip, right on the spot where he had been hit by the truck. Swan yelled and rolled off Rhodes.

Rhodes used the last of his agility in getting up and kicking Swan in the same place where he had hit him. Swan yelled again.

Rhodes knew that he wasn't being very sporting, and he didn't really care, not even if Swan's hip was fractured.

Then he heard the pickup start. He turned to face it, looking for a way to jump, but it wasn't necessary. This time Betsy Higgins had no intention of running over him. She backed up and started the other way, out of the yard and down the road.

Rhodes looked at Swan, who didn't seem eager to go anywhere, then limped over to his own car. He called Hack and told him to alert the deputies to be on the lookout for the pickup.

After he described it, Hack asked, "What's the license number?"

Rhodes didn't say anything for a second. "I don't know," he finally said.

It was Hack's turn to be quiet for a while. "I'll get it right on the air," he said then.

"Good," Rhodes said. "And tell Lawton I'm bringing in a prisoner."

"Oh," Hack said. "Then not everybody got away."

"Not quite," Rhodes said.

There wasn't much fight left in Phil Swan, and when they got to the jail Rhodes had to help him out of the car and into the building. After they booked him, Lawton helped him upstairs while Hack called Dr. White.

"Tell the truth," Hack said, hanging up the phone, "you look a lot worse than your prisoner."

Rhodes looked at his hands, front and back. "I guess I could use some Mercurochrome," he said.

"We got a spray for stuff like that now," Hack said, rummaging around in his desk drawer. "Specially for big places like that." He came up with an aerosol can and tossed it to Rhodes.

Rhodes caught it, removed the cap, and sprayed it on his hands. It was cool and didn't burn.

"Shoulda washed them first," Hack said.

Rhodes tossed him the can, which Hack returned to the drawer.

"Gonna have to wash your clothes," Hack said.

"I do that anyway," Rhodes said.

"Yeah. Notice anything different?"

Rhodes, whose mind had been otherwise occupied, looked around the office for the first time. "Ho Ho Ho," he said.

Under the gunrack was a short but shapely Christmas tree, hung with blue ornaments and strung with blue lights. The lights were not plugged in.

"Miz Daniel brought it by at lunch time," Hack said. "Said she might have some presents to put under it later."

"Uh-oh," Rhodes said.

"What I thought," Hack said. "You ain't bought her a thing, have you?"

"I've been busy," Rhodes said.

"If I was you, I'd get un-busy long enough to buy that woman a present," Hack said. "I swear, sometimes I don't think you deserve her."

"Sometimes I feel the same way," Rhodes said.

Just then Dr. White came in and saved him from having to say more.

Rhodes took White up to the prisoner and then came back down. "Anybody called in about Betsy Higgins?" he asked.

"Nope," Hack said. "Not a peep."

Rhodes thought about going out to look himself, but she

73

could have been well out of the county by now, or on any one of a hundred back roads. Then he thought about lunch, which he'd missed again. He wondered why it was that he could miss so many lunches and still not lose any weight. If he couldn't lose, he might as well eat.

"I'm going out for a bite," he told Hack. "I'll be back to question Swan in a little while."

"You think he might have to go to the hospital?" Hack asked.

"I'm not sure. Maybe he just has a bad bruise, but if the doctor says send him, do it. I can talk to him there."

"You gonna look for a present while you're out?"

"I'll think about it," Rhodes said.

Chapter 9

RHODES DIDN'T LOOK for a present. Instead he went by the 7-11 and bought a loaf of wholewheat bread, a package of bologna, some sliced cheese (each slice individually wrapped), and a six-pack of Dr. Pepper in nonreturnable bottles. Then he went home.

On his way to his house he called Hack on the radio and asked him to have Ruth Grady interview the Martins' neighbors and try to find out who their friends were. Although he had a suspect in jail, he didn't want to neglect other possibilities.

While he sat at his kitchen table moodily chewing on his bologna sandwich, Rhodes considered his health. The bologna was full of additives and fats, the cheese wasn't even cheese at all but a mixture of ingredients called "pasteurized process cheese food," and the soft drink was full of sugar. At least the bread was stone ground. That was supposed to hold in the vitamins or something. Maybe he should go in after eating and give the bicycle a try.

He wondered what his problem was, and decided that it was the fact that he was engaged. Or sort of. He still didn't think that he was *really* engaged. A man who's been married once doesn't get "engaged." Or at least Rhodes didn't think so. He was out of his depth. He tried to think of what Cary Grant would do. When Grant had hired Sophia Loren to take care of his children in *Houseboat*, he had fallen in love with her. Rhodes remembered that much. But had he given her a ring? Had he gotten down on his knees and pleaded for her hand? Details like that had slipped Rhodes's mind.

Rhodes got up from the table, scraped the crumbs into his hand, then tossed them in the sink. He took the last swallow of his Dr Pepper and threw the bottle in the trash. Maybe he forgot details because he wanted to forget them. Wasn't that what psychiatrists said? He didn't think it was true, but he knew that it was at least a possibility.

Details. They were always important in any investigation of any crime, and it was funny how often you overlooked them, even the most obvious ones. But it wasn't as if they were forgotten, or never noticed in the first place. Sometimes the details suddenly jumped into your mind, coming all at once out of whatever dark corner they'd been hiding in, and made everything clear. Maybe things would work out like that in the Martin case, which was still bothering Rhodes. It wasn't easy to think about murder and a missing man when your mind was on being engaged. Or it could have been the other way around. It wasn't easy to think about being engaged when your mind was on murder and a missing man.

Rhodes gave it up. He went out back, fed Speedo, and drove back to the jail.

On his way to the jail Rhodes drove through the downtown to see if it looked any cheerier in the daylight. It was too warm for Christmas, but people must be getting the spirit somehow.

The streets were not crowded, but there were a few people walking in and out of the stores, some of them even carrying packages wrapped in green, red and white paper. Seeing them didn't cheer Rhodes up, and he didn't stop to look in any of the stores himself.

76

The jail didn't look any more cheerful on the outside, and the tree didn't help the inside much either. A jail was a jail.

Hack and Lawton were talking when Rhodes walked in. They got suddenly quiet.

Rhodes looked at them, but they didn't say anything. They just looked at him.

Finally Rhodes said, "Did you send Ruth Grady to the Martins' neighborhood?"

"Sure did," Hack said. "Right after she got through at Hubbard's."

"Hubbard's?"

"That's right," Lawton said. "She had some trouble—"

"*She* didn't have any trouble," Hack said, seizing control again. He didn't want Lawton to have any of the story. "It was Hubbard that called us. He had the trouble."

Hubbard, Rhodes knew, was Ted Hubbard, who had a department store just off the main street. It had been in his family for over a hundred years and was one of the few really nice stores in town. It didn't make nearly as much money as it once did, or so Rhodes had heard, but if you wanted to buy nice clothes or shoes, some of the real name brands anyway, it was the only place in Blacklin County to shop. Otherwise you had to drive to one of the cities that were not too far away.

"What kind of trouble?" Rhodes asked.

"Nothin' much," Hack said.

"Oh," Rhodes said and waited.

"Had some trouble with his Santy Claus," Lawton said.

"That ain't right," Hack said. "He didn't have no trouble with his Santy Claus."

"Yes, he did," Lawton said. "He—"

"No, he didn't," Hack said. "It was a kid who caused the trouble."

"A kid," Rhodes said, trying to track the direction of the conversation.

"Yeah," Hack said. "You remember that Terrell kid?"

"He's the one that tried to tie the cans to Miz Coppard's cat's tail," Lawton said helpfully.

"I remember him," Rhodes said. He would have been

77

willing to bet that Miz Coppard's cat was never the same after that. Miz Coppard, either, for that matter. She really liked her cats.

"Yeah, him," Hack said. "Anyway, he went in the store with his mama, and she wanted to get his picture made with Santy Claus."

Rhodes recalled reading in the local paper that Hubbard had for the first time in the store's history offered youngsters the opportunity to have their photos made sitting in the lap of "that jolly old elf from the North Pole, Santa Claus himself, photos made with the same attention to quality that has made Hubbard's a byword in Clearview for over 100 years." Rhodes had thought that maybe Hubbard was overstating things, since the photo was nothing more than a shot with a Polaroid camera, and Hubbard's was charging $5.00 a shot.

"I always wanted to have me a picture made with Santy Claus," Lawton said, "except they didn't do that when I was a kid."

"Yeah," Hack said. "Back then we was lucky to even get anything for Christmas, except maybe an orange or a hick'ry nut. Sometimes two hick'ry nuts if we'd been real good."

"I got a little toy truck once, Hack," Lawton said. "It was a little bitty one, but I remember it was red. That was the best thing I ever got. I played with it all day, and then my brother beat me up and took it."

"About the Terrell kid," Rhodes said.

"I bet he gets all kind of presents," Lawton said. "He wouldn't even pay attention to a little bitty old truck like that one I got. I bet he wouldn't have the least idea what to do with a hick'ry nut."

"Kids today get ever' kind of a thing," Hack said. "Those whatchamacallems—Transformers. And those Masters of the Universe."

"I remember I was glad just to get a piece of gum," Lawton said. "I guess I got about one piece a year. I remember there was a nail in the wall by my bed, and ever' night I'd stick my gum on the head of that nail so I could chew it the next day. It had to last a long time."

"I believe," Hack said. "Why, at my house—"

78

"The Terrell kid," Rhodes said again. He almost hated to break in. When Hack and Lawton got started in a competition telling of how much they'd been deprived in their childhoods, the stories were always funny, if not always true.

"Oh, yeah, him," Hack said. "He assaulted Santy Claus."

"Assaulted?"

"Yeah, but Miz Grady—Ruth—didn't arrest him," Lawton said.

"Wasn't any use, him bein' a juvenile and all," Hack said. "Besides, Santy deserved it."

"Deserved to be assaulted?" Rhodes found that a little hard to believe.

"He hit the kid," Hack said. "Least that's what his mama says. If it's true, I don't know as I blame Santy too much. Kid probably needed it."

"Why?"

"He kicked Santy in the shins, the way Santy tells it." Hack seemed to think that was all that needed to be said.

Rhodes just waited.

"He didn't get the car he wanted last year," Lawton said.

"Toy car?" Rhodes asked.

"Trans-Am," Hack said. "Red Trans-Am. Hell, the kid's nine years old, nearly. He needs a Trans-Am."

"So he kicked the Hubbard Santa?"

"Right. Just walked right up there and whaled him in the shins. Santy jumped up and grabbed him. Don't much blame him. Whole day of havin' to sit there and listen to those little farts tell him about what they want for Christmas. I don't think he hit him, though."

"But the mother does?"

"Not really. She was just afraid her kid would get tossed in the slammer. Wanted to stir up the water."

"Slammer?" Rhodes said.

"That's what Ruth said she called it. Folks watch too many TV shows," Hack said.

"But everything's all right now?"

"Yeah. Lots of little kids standin' around cryin' and takin' on for a while, but Ruth got things straight. They was all

79

afraid Santy was goin' to slide down the chimbly this year and kick their butts. Do 'em a world of good, you ask me.'' Hack was not overly fond of children at the best of times. Christmas always brought out the worst in him.

"Maybe I should check by there," Rhodes said.

"I wouldn't," Lawton said. "It's all right now. Those kids see the Sheriff come in, they might all break and run for the hills.''

"You may be right," Rhodes said.

"I bet I am," Lawton said. "Now if you wanted to buy a present . . ."

"Don't start that," Rhodes said.

Hack and Lawton said nothing. They simply looked at him accusingly.

Rhodes looked away first. "What about Phil Swan?" he asked.

"He's all right," Hack said. "Doc said to leave him here. He'll have a nice bruise, be a little sore, but that's all."

Rhodes was already feeling more than a little sore himself. "I'll go up and talk to him, then," he said. "Maybe he can clear up some things."

"He ain't real friendly," Lawton said. Lawton liked to talk to the prisoners, and usually they liked him. He wasn't sympathetic, exactly, but he was always willing to listen to their stories.

Rhodes went up to the cellblock. Swan was sitting on his bunk, staring through the bars of his door.

"Looks like your ladyfriend ran out on you," Rhodes said. "Tried to run *over* you, for that matter."

Swan continued to stare through the bars as if Rhodes weren't there. He flexed his hands once, as if he was thinking about taking hold of the steel and bending it to allow himself room to step through. Looking at the size of his hands, Rhodes wouldn't have bet against him.

"She tried to run you down, you know," Rhodes said.

"It was an accident," Swan said. "She wouldn't do that."

"Maybe," Rhodes said. "Maybe not."

Swan just snorted, like a horse pawing the ground.

"You want to talk about it?" Rhodes asked.

80

"Nothing to talk about," Swan said. "You might as well let me go."

"Let you go?" Rhodes asked. "You kidding me?"

"You can't hold me without a charge," Swan said. "I'll be out of here before you can say Jack Spratt."

"Don't count on it," Rhodes said. "I'm charging you with assault." He tried to keep from grinning as he thought of the Terrell boy.

"You came on my property," Swan said.

"No," Rhodes said. "It's Dr. Martin's property. Or, if you pressed the definitions, it could be called Betsy Higgins's property, since the rent is in her name. But not yours."

"Same difference," Swan said.

"The judge won't see it that way," Rhodes said.

"I guess you know the judge." Swan turned away and lay on the bunk. It was much too small for him, and his feet hung off the end. He didn't seem to mind.

"The judge might want to know why you were so ready to fight," Rhodes said. "He might wonder if you were trying to keep me from finding out something."

"Maybe," Swan said. "Like I said, you know the judge."

"So will you, before long," Rhodes said. "You might be getting to know a lawyer, too, and after that some of the residents of our better prisons. Maybe you read about them in *Newsweek*."

"I don't read much," Swan said.

"Did you see the little old lady out walking when you were at Martin's house?" Rhodes asked.

"What old lady?" Swan asked. "I haven't been anywhere."

Rhodes had hoped to catch Swan off guard, but it hadn't worked. "Your pickup was seen," he said. "The one with the bullriding sign in the back window."

"Lots of them signs around," Swan said.

"Probably not in trucks like yours," Rhodes told him. "And the lady may be able to identify you. You could help yourself out by telling me why you were over there. Maybe we can get the charge reduced to manslaughter."

"Charge?" Swan sat up. "What charge?"

81

"Capital murder," Rhodes said. "You killed Mrs. Martin during the commission of a burglary. That makes you eligible for a lethal injection. I hear it's not a bad way to go, though."

Swan got off the bunk, walked over to the bars, and wrapped his thick fingers around them. "I didn't kill anybody," he said.

"Maybe not. But if there's a crowbar in that truck of yours, we'll find it. And if there's bloodstains on it, you're probably a goner."

"Now wait a minute," Swan said. "You're gettin' a little ahead of yourself here. Maybe I've got a crowbar, but that don't mean I killed anybody with it."

"Then you don't have a thing to worry about," Rhodes said. "Maybe it was your girlfriend that did it. You might want to save that point in case you have to plea bargain with the D.A."

"Now hold on. You can't even prove I was there."

"I've got that lady who saw your truck, though."

Swan's hands gripped the bars so tightly that his knuckles were getting white. "I wasn't there," he said.

"You told me that already," Rhodes said. "Maybe you're even telling the truth. But I think I've got enough to go to the Grand Jury with right now. I've got a motive, I've got a witness, I've got you assaulting an officer. I figure the Grand Jury will indict you without a second thought. After that it's anybody's guess. You're going to be mighty unhappy for a long time, no matter what. Unless you just like jail a lot."

"Listen, Sheriff, I—"

"You don't have to tell me a thing," Rhodes said. He went on to tell Swan his rights. Apparently Swan was not so fond of jail that he wanted to stay any longer than he had to. Rhodes had painted the picture as black as possible in the hopes of breaking Swan down and finding out more than he knew already. It looked as if Swan was just dumb enough or scared enough to cooperate.

"I want to tell you," Swan said, "me and Betsy didn't kill anybody."

"But you were there, weren't you." Rhodes said.

Swan relaxed his hold on the bars and went back to sit on the bunk. His head sagged, and he didn't look up. "Yeah, we were there. I guess that old lady saw us, all right. But we didn't kill anybody."

"Didn't steal anything, either, I guess."

"No, we didn't steal anything. We didn't want anything those people had."

"All right," Rhodes said. "Let's say I believe you so far. How did Mrs. Martin get dead if you didn't do it?"

Swan looked up at him through the bars. "I don't know," he said. "She was already dead when we got there."

Chapter 10

RHODES SHOOK HIS HEAD. "I'm sorry you said that. I thought you could do better."

"It's the truth," Swan said. "Listen, I've been in the pen before. I don't want to go back there if I don't have to, and I'm not goin' for somethin' I didn't do."

Rhodes didn't know that Swan had been in prison before, but he would have found out soon enough. The fact that he had a record would make him look even worse to the Grand Jury. He mentioned the fact to Swan.

"Jesus, I know that. But this time I'm tellin' the truth."

"Well," Rhodes said, "try it on me for size, and we'll see how it fits."

"O.K.," Swan said. He launched into his story.

It seemed that Betsy Higgins had a small savings account at one of the local banks. She hadn't wanted to touch the money, but Swan was out of work and so was she. Swan hoped to get on soon at the local cable plant, but for a while there wouldn't be any income, at least not enough to pay the rent. So Betsy had finally agreed to dip into the savings. They had gotten the money, but then there had been another argument. Betsy had wanted to wait one more day. Swan wanted to pay the money before Martin came back and tried to take the TV set again, or tried to get them evicted, which he had threatened to do.

After arguing most of the afternoon, they agreed to go out for supper and spend a little of the money on themselves, then to take the rent by Martin's house. When they got there it was already getting dark, but the garage light was on. Betsy had stayed in the truck while Swan took the money to the door. He knocked loudly several times, but no one came. Then he noticed that the door was slightly ajar. He gave it a push.

"Thought you might go in and see what you could see, huh?" Rhodes said.

"Not exactly," Swan said. "I thought maybe someone was there and just wouldn't come. Some folks don't like to come to the door, you know?"

Rhodes didn't blame them, not if someone like Swan was at the door. But someone like that wouldn't leave the door ajar, either. Rhodes let the point pass, and Swan went on.

"I walked into the kitchen—you've seen that kitchen? I never saw so many gadgets in my life. I bet there's a fortune tied up in that kitchen."

"I'm not interested in the kitchen," Rhodes said.

"Yeah, I guess not. Well, I just went in a couple of steps and then I saw her, lyin' on the floor. I stood there a minute, just lookin'. I was spooked. I never saw anybody dead like that before."

Rhodes put a hand up to cover the beginnings of a smile. Like a lot of big, tough-looking men, Swan was as much bluster as action. Oh, he would try to wring somebody's pipsqueak neck, but his toughness didn't go much further than that. He was beginning to believe that Swan was telling the truth.

"So anyway, I looked, and then I got out of there. I was scared. I got in the truck and we took off."

"You were about to take off again," Rhodes said.

Swan stared at him. "Huh?"

"When I came to the house," Rhodes said.

85

"Oh," Swan said. "Yeah. Well, we figured maybe somebody had found the body by then, and we knew you were already on our case. We just decided to head on out."

Rhodes thought about it. In a way it all made sense, especially if Swan already had a record. He wouldn't want to hang around and get picked up. Ex-convicts didn't always get the benefit of the doubt.

"What about Betsy Higgins?" Rhodes asked.

"I don't know," Swan said. "I didn't think she'd just take off and leave me like that. Hell, she's got my truck."

"You want to press charges?"

For a minute, Swan hesitated, and Rhodes thought he might actually be considering it. Then he said, "Naw, I guess not. She was just scared, I guess."

Rhodes left it at that and went back down to the office. The more he thought about it, the more he was convinced that Swan wasn't lying. Still, he would've liked to get his hands on the pickup and see if there happened to be a crowbar in it. And if there was, he'd like to send it to a good lab for examination.

"What do you think?" Hack asked when Rhodes came through the door.

"I don't know," Rhodes said. "I'm not sure he's guilty of a thing, except maybe running away when he should have stood his ground."

"If he ain't, who is?"

"Well," Rhodes said, "that's what we have to find out."

"Not me," Hack said. "I just answer the phone. You're the lawman around here."

Rhodes was about to offer a mild argument when Ruth Grady came in. She had a white paper bag in one hand. "Hi, everybody," she said.

"What's in the bag?" Rhodes asked.

"Doughnuts. You know that little shop that just opened up over on Peach Street?"

Rhodes had driven by the place, a little prefab wooden building that hadn't even been painted. "I've seen it," he said.

"They have great doughnuts." Ruth was not fat, but she

86

was not thin, either. She enjoyed doughnuts, cake, and candy. "I brought these for Hack."

Hack had a sweet tooth, too. At first he had not at all liked the idea of a woman deputy, but Ruth had won him over with a combination of her abilities, her cheerful attitude, and a series of bribes in the form of cakes and other goodies. "That was nice of you to think of me," he said. He looked at Rhodes. "It's more than I can say of some folks."

Ruth handed Hack the bag. "Look at the pretty tree," she said, noticing it for the first time.

Hack had opened the bag and was peering inside. "Might be some presents under it later," he said. He reached into the bag and brought out a jelly-filled doughnut. "My favorite kind. Raspberry." He bit into it, and jelly squirted out one side and got on his fingers.

"They're napkins inside the sack," Ruth said.

Hack put the doughnut down on his desk and reached back into the bag, bringing out a napkin. He wiped his fingers, picked up the doughnut, and wiped the spot on his desk.

"What kind of presents," Ruth asked.

"All kinds," Hack said. "I ain't sure."

"I think it's a good idea," Ruth said. "Should we draw names?"

Rhodes felt as if things were getting out of hand in some way. "Draw names?"

"So we can get a gift for the one whose name we draw," Ruth said. "It might be fun."

Hack wiped his mouth with the napkin. The doughnut had disappeared. "I think we did that in school when I was a kid," he said. "That was a while ago, I'll tell you."

Rhodes didn't know why he wasn't in the Christmas spirit. Maybe it was the weather. Maybe it was the murder of Mrs. Martin and the disappearance of her husband. Or maybe it was the fact that he didn't have a present for Ivy Daniel. He didn't want to try to figure it out.

"I'm not sure we'll have time for that," he said.

"Sure we will," Hack said. "We don't have any crime on Christmas Day, 'cept maybe a drunk or two. We got plenty of time."

"Good," Ruth said. "I'll write all the names on slips of paper and we can draw."

"How about the Martins' neighbors?" Rhodes asked, trying to change the subject.

"Oh," Ruth said. "Sure. I need to talk to you about that."

"Don't mind me," Hack said. "I'm just an old man who's good for eatin' doughnuts. You can talk in front of me."

Rhodes had to laugh. "Old man, my foot. You could probably outrun either one of us. And you know you want to hear every word of this."

Hack ignored him, reaching for another doughnut.

Ruth explained what she'd found out. "Apparently the Martins don't socialize much, at least not around that neighborhood. All Dr. Martin is interested in is buying old houses and fixing them up for rent property. At least, that's what most of the neighbors think. You know that area—not many houses, and the ones there aren't too close to each other. I got most of this from a Mrs. Stone, Scottie Stone. She lives in what you'd call the house next door if it weren't a half block away."

"I know the one," Rhodes said. "Brownish brick, shake shingles."

"That's it. This Mrs. Stone—she insisted that I should call her Scottie—is a member of the Garden Club and the Rotary Anns and the Friday Club and just about every other club in town. Mrs. Martin wasn't in a one of them. A lot of the women resent that, what with all the money the Martins make. They ought to be 'contributing to the community.' "

"But they aren't," Rhodes said.

"Not a bit. All Mrs. Martin does is sit around the house all day, at least according to Scottie. Sometimes she comes out—*came* out—and worked in the yard a little, but that was it."

"That's not much help," Rhodes said.

"Well, there's one other thing. Scottie has the impression that the Martins weren't getting along too well."

"That might be interesting," Rhodes said. "What gave her that impression?"

"You know the kind of weather we've been having this

88

winter, kind of cool at night but pretty warm during the day? Except for that last cold snap, I mean.''

"Sure," Rhodes said. "So?"

"So everybody leaves their windows up most of the time, except at night. Scottie heard them yelling in the late afternoons."

"She hear anything specific?"

"Well, she thought she heard Mrs. Martin yell something about—" Ruth stopped and sneaked a look at Hack, who was studiously ignoring them "—about someone she called 'that bitch.' "

Rhodes sneaked a look at Hack as well. Hack wouldn't like the idea of a woman using such language. He was a real Texan.

Since Hack was still ignoring them and apparently hadn't heard, Rhodes got to work trying to think of someone who might seem like a bitch to Mrs. Martin. The name of Betsy Higgins came to mind almost at once. Could Martin have had something going with her? Could the blowup in the office, and the whole thing about the curse, have been some sort of cover-up? It was possible, Rhodes supposed, but Betsy hadn't seemed like Dr. Martin's type. Still, if there was one thing that Rhodes had learned in his career, it was that you could never, *never*, tell what someone's type might be.

"She hear anything else?" Rhodes asked.

"No," Ruth said, "and I sort of got the impression that she was really trying. I wouldn't be surprised if she went out in the yard and listened. She seemed really curious about the whole thing."

That didn't surprise Rhodes. There was nothing like a crime to get people's curiosity aroused. Just seeing an officer in the area was enough to stall traffic, whether you were in a small town or a big city.

"I wonder . . ." Rhodes said.

"What?"

"Nothing. I've got enough on the prisoner upstairs to hold him for a while. I was just thinking that the story he told me might not be as truthful as I thought it was."

In fact, Rhodes was thinking that Swan might have been

a better liar than he'd given him credit for. It was certainly a possibility that he was lying to protect Betsy Higgins, especially if the two had been involved in some sort of scam to get something from Martin, a scam based on some relationship between Martin and Higgins. It was something he'd have to devote more thought to.

"You have anything else for me?" Ruth asked.

"Not right now," Rhodes said. "You working on anything in particular?"

"Just that hot check case. Another one turned up today."

"Forgot to tell you about that," Hack said. He'd been listening all along.

"Any leads on that?" Rhodes asked.

"I've got an informant who wants to talk to me about it," Ruth said. "We'll see what he has."

"Good," Rhodes said. "Keep after that. I'll get in touch if I need anything else on this Martin business." He turned to look at Hack, but he didn't say anything.

"Anybody can forget," Hack said. "I got a lot on my mind. Besides, I'm an old man. Can't expect much from an old man."

Rhodes still didn't say anything. Hack had a mind like a teenager.

"I got to worry about whose name I'm gonna draw," Hack said. "That's a problem, too. I got a lot on my mind."

"I'll write down the names and leave them in a bowl or something on your desk," Ruth said. "When the deputies come in, they can draw."

"Good idea," Hack said.

"Think you can remember to tell them about it?" Rhodes asked.

Hack glared at him.

It was getting late afternoon when Rhodes left the jail. The air was crisp, but not cold. He wondered how much longer the good weather could possibly last. It was December, after all. He wished he'd had a chance to get by Little Barnes's place and try out that tank, which was no doubt full of fish eager to bite the first hook presented to them. He knew bet-

90

ter, of course. There never was a tank like that, but every fisherman liked to think that the one he hadn't fished in was the one that would prove to be the exception.

Rhodes got in his car and drove toward the house where Betsy Higgins and Swan had lived. There was always the chance that Betsy had come back. After all, her TV was there and probably most of her clothes and other worldly goods, whatever those might be.

The pickup was nowhere to be seen as Rhodes drove down the street, but he stopped anyway. He got out of the car and looked at the house. If Swan and Higgins *had* been responsible for Martin's disappearance, then where was Martin?

In the house?

Buried in the yard?

Neither possibility was very likely. There were all too many places in Blacklin County where a body could be dumped and never seen again, except by accident.

Rhodes remembered an old movie that he had enjoyed, *The Trouble with Harry*, in which a body had been found in the woods somewhere. Vermont? He couldn't remember exactly. Various members of the cast had dragged it here and there, trying to dispose of it.

It had been funny in the movie, but it wouldn't be funny if it were really happening, if Martin's body were somewhere out there being dragged from place to place.

That opened up a new train of thought.

What if there wasn't a body?

All along Rhodes had been considering things from the angle that Martin had not only disappeared but was dead. Why did he think that?

Rhodes started off to the west where the sun was about a half hour from going down, turning the few clouds in that part of the sky a grayish pink. The slight chill came through his shirt, and he wished he'd put on his windbreaker.

Why did he think Martin was dead? Well, it sure seemed that nobody liked the man. Little Barnes didn't. Swan didn't. Betsy Higgins didn't. Or she didn't seem to. Rhodes wasn't ready to clear her on that count yet, not considering the words that Mrs. Stone thought she had heard.

Martin's office staff seemed to like him, though. Tammy, Carol, Jamie. They were all pretty torn up over the whole thing. Rhodes thought about his talk with them. There was something there, he thought, something he might have missed. He went over the scene in his mind, but he couldn't quite figure out what it was that was bothering him.

He looked at the house again. It was neat and well kept. Martin must have been a man who took pride in his property, and Swan—or Betsy Higgins—hadn't let things go the way renters sometimes did, those who thought that after all the property wasn't theirs and never would be, so why bother taking care of it?

Rhodes thought he heard something from inside the house.

He caught himself staring at the front door, as if his eyes could help him to hear better.

A minute passed with no further evidence of a sound. Rhodes had begun to think that he'd heard something from one of the other houses nearby. Then it came again, a faint bump of some kind.

Rhodes moved away from his car and up toward the front door. He knocked, but there was no answer from inside.

Rhodes felt for his sidearm. It was there, as usual, in its thumb-release holster, but he didn't draw it. He didn't like to use weapons if it wasn't necessary, and if it hadn't been necessary with Swan, it shouldn't be necessary now. Most of the time, Rhodes thought, guns just got in the way, and sometimes they were downright dangerous. Sometimes they were dangerous to the wrong people, and he had reason to know that, too.

He walked around to the side of the house and stood listening by the windows.

Nothing.

He went on around to the back door, the door through which Swan and Betsy Higgins had tried to make their getaway earlier. The door was slightly ajar.

The sun was dropping lower now, almost to the horizon. There was a definite chill in the air, and in a few minutes it would be getting dark.

No lights showed in the house, not from any of the windows Rhodes had passed or the back door. If he waited any longer to go in, whoever was in there would have an advantage—assuming that whoever was in there was familiar with the arrangement of the furniture, and Rhodes was assuming that the "whoever" was Betsy Higgins.

On the other hand, maybe one of the neighborhood kids, someone who had seen the earlier incident, had decided to slip in and see what he could find, figuring that Swan wouldn't be back anytime soon to stop him.

There were three cement steps, the kind you buy at the lumber yard, leading to the doorway. Rhodes stepped up on the top one, pulled open the screen, and pushed the slightly open wooden door.

As the door swung silently inward, Rhodes drew his pistol. He didn't like it, but he really didn't want to enter the house without it. He'd had experience doing that, too.

He stepped into the kitchen. It was much darker on the inside than it had been outside, even with the door open. Rhodes could make out a table and four chairs, the cabinets, the stove, and the refrigerator. There was no one in the room, and no more noise from anywhere in the house.

He stood quietly for a minute, listening. He was almost certain that someone was doing the same in another room, standing silently and listening to him.

He looked through a doorway into the dark shadows of the living room. No one there, at least no one he could see.

He walked through the doorway and went through it fast, just like in the movies, whirling around, his gun ready.

There was nobody there.

He felt a little foolish, and he knew that he hadn't been able to make the move quietly. If there really was someone else in the house, whoever it was knew where he was located for sure.

The other door led to a short hall and the two bedrooms. The back bedroom would be where the TV set was. If Betsy Higgins had come back for anything, it would be the TV. How she was planning to get it out to the pickup, wherever she had parked it, Rhodes had no idea, but he was convinced that she was in the back room.

He went into the hall, as quietly as he could this time, getting his back to the wall opposite the door and keeping his eyes toward the back of the house.

The sun must have been completely below the horizon by now. It seemed very dark to Rhodes. He waited, hoping that his eyes would adjust, but it didn't help much.

He edged along the wall, glancing in the open bathroom door as he passed. More darkness, but nothing moving.

When he got to the door into the back bedroom, he took a deep breath, squared himself into the hallway, and prepared to go through.

That was when he heard the noise behind him.

He tried to turn, but by then it was too late.

Something hit him in the back like a runaway dump truck.

Chapter 11

RHODES WAS FORCED forward into the bedroom. The force of the blow caused him to drop the pistol, which skittered across the floor and bumped into a wall.

When he recovered from his initial surprise, Rhodes was even more surprised to discover that whatever had hit him was still there, hanging on to his neck and shoulders, pummeling his head and pulling his hair.

He tried to shake loose, but whatever was on him was sticking to him just like one of those little sticker burrs from a sandy land hill. There wasn't much weight there, but there was plenty of tenacity.

The fury of it all finally bore Rhodes to the floor, where he was able to roll over and get a grip on Betsy Higgins's wrists before she beat him black and blue, at least in the area of the face. First Swan and now this. It hadn't been a good day at all.

He held on to the wrists until Betsy Higgins began to tire, though it wasn't easy. He wouldn't have thought she had that much energy in her, but while she wasn't big, she was certainly wiry. She thrashed and flopped like a catfish on a tank dam on a sunny day.

When he could finally get a breath, Rhodes said, "You've got to calm down, Miz Higgins. Nobody's going to hurt you."

"You're going to, if you can," she said, getting out the words between gasping for breath and trying to spit on him. "You had a gun in your hand."

Rhodes managed to push her away slightly and get to his knees, still keeping his grip. "I didn't know for sure it was you in here," he said.

"You wanted to kill me," Higgins said, kicking, squirming, pulling with that wiry strength. It was all Rhodes could do to hold on.

"I just don't want you to kill *me*," Rhodes said. "It seems like you're still trying."

Suddenly Betsy Higgins stopped moving. She grew rigid as a rock and threw back her head. "By the name of Lucifer," she cried out, "by the name of—"

Rhodes couldn't understand the names she called out then. They sounded something like "Ah-hee-yay" and "Eh-gla," but he wasn't very good at the language of witchcraft.

"—I command you to release me." Then she started to struggle fiercely again.

Rhodes held on. Apparently the spell wasn't going to work.

"I call upon you and your house a plague of demons!" she shouted. "By all sacred names, by the name of—"

Rhodes didn't like to hit a woman, but he decided that was the only way he could shut Betsy Higgins up. Besides, she was proving almost more than he could hold on to. He risked letting go of one wrist, pulling back his right hand to tap her on the jaw.

She didn't give him a chance. She swung her left hand faster than Rhodes would have thought she could, and with more power, hitting him flush on the nose.

He felt something crunch and the first hot flow of blood. He reached and grabbed her wrist before she could swing again, but he realized that it was just a lucky grab. She was not only fast, she was faster than he was. Rhodes felt vaguely the same way he had felt the day he'd found out that Ivy

Daniel could ride a motorcycle and he couldn't. He wasn't going to take any more chances. He started dragging Betsy Higgins down the hall.

It wasn't easy. It was dark, and he couldn't see. Besides, he was having to walk backwards. And of course Betsy wasn't coming along without a fight. She hooked her feet on the door frame; then when Rhodes pulled her away from that, she managed to hook them in the bathroom doorway.

They went through the house like that, Rhodes occasionally bumping into something like a chair or a wall, Betsy hooking her feet on anything that came in her path.

Finally he got her out in the yard. As he dragged her around the house, she began to scream. "Help! Rape! Rape! Murder! Rape!" The thin voice was a falsetto screech.

Rhodes could hear doors opening in the nearby houses, and he even saw a porch light come on, but no one came too close. Most of them had already spotted his car in front of the house earlier, peeking from behind window shades and curtains. They weren't about to interfere.

He got Betsy to the county car and this time did not let go. He got hold of both wrists with his right hand and opened the door to the backseat with his left. She almost managed to pull away, but he held on. When the door was open wide enough, he shoved her roughly inside, without regard for her head or body. It wasn't good procedure, but it got the job done.

When he slammed the door behind her, she threw herself at it. She hit it so hard that Rhodes was momentarily surprised that it held. It seemed almost to bulge out at him like the door of a car in a Merrie Melodies cartoon.

He walked around and got in the driver's seat. Betsy was rattling the metal grille between them furiously, spitting and cursing and calling on strange names, none of which Rhodes could have pronounced. He wasn't worried about the grille. If the door held, so would the grille. He got on the radio and called Hack, asking him to get in touch with Ruth Grady and have her waiting at the jail.

Then he went back in the house to retrieve his pistol. This time he turned on the lights and went into the front room.

97

He had been mistaken about where the TV was located. It was in the front, along with a king-size waterbed.

Betsy Higgins had brought a small dolly made of red-painted metal into the room. Rhodes had seen them for sale at Wal-Mart. She had managed to get the TV set down off the stand where it rested and onto the floor. The lip of the dolly was slid under it. No doubt the bumps he had heard were made by Betsy as she struggled with the set. She probably intended to wheel it out the back door and on to wherever she had parked the pickup.

When Rhodes got back to the car, Betsy had stopped struggling. She was curled up in a corner of the back seat with her legs under her, staring at him. He hoped she didn't have a weapon. He hadn't searched her, but that was a job for Ruth Grady. He figured that if she had been carrying anything dangerous, she would have used it on him in the house instead of jumping him, though, so he felt relatively safe.

He started the car and drove away.

Ruth Grady was waiting when he got to the jail, and she went to the car with him to get the prisoner. Betsy didn't try to escape. Instead she went docilely into the building.

Rhodes charged her with assaulting an officer and sent her to the partitioned-off ''women's cell'' to be searched.

"Damn," Hack said when Ruth and the prisoner were gone. "You look like you've been kicked in the snoot by a mule."

Rhodes looked down at his shirt. There was dried blood on it, and he could feel the blood in his nose. "At least Ruth was polite enough not to mention it," he said.

"Prob'ly afraid for her job," Hack said. "You better get cleaned up. Ivy's comin' down here."

Rhodes touched his nose. It felt big and tender, like a very overripe tomato. "What for?" he asked.

"Bringin' some presents, she said."

Rhodes wondered if his nose was broken. Probably not. It didn't hurt enough for that. But it was definitely damaged. "All right," he said. "I'll try to wash some of this off."

He went into the restroom in back of the office. He managed to wash most of the blood off his face and out of his nose, but of course it wouldn't come out of his shirt. The cold water felt good on his face, so he stuck his whole head under the faucet and let the water run through his hair and over his neck.

He came out, drying his face and hair with a dark brown towel.

"Prob'ly the only clean towel we got," Hack said.

"Hard to tell for sure," Rhodes said.

"Yeah," Hack said. "That's why I got the brown ones. I imagine we got a big wash load of 'em in the hamper, though."

Rhodes knew what he meant. "I'll take care of it," he said.

As he was putting the towel back on the rack, Ivy walked in, her hands full of presents.

"It's Miz Santy Claus," Hack said. He got up from his chair. "Let me help you with those."

Together they stacked the presents under the tree while Rhodes watched. The ones wrapped in foil sparkled in the light.

When they were finished, Ivy turned and looked at Rhodes. "What happened?" she asked.

"That's what I asked him," Hack said. "He got snippy with me."

Ivy walked over to Rhodes and put her hand on his cheek. "Santa's nose is supposed to be like a cherry," she said. "Not a tomato."

Rhodes laughed. "It should look more like a cherry in a couple of days. Right now it feels like a basketball."

"We get a lot of tough customers," Hack said.

"Don't listen to him," Rhodes said. He told her about the encounter with Betsy Higgins.

"You ought to be more careful," she said. "We want you to be around to open your presents."

"We're drawing names," Rhodes said. "You didn't have to bring so many."

"They aren't much. Just a little something for everybody I know. Besides, I like buying presents."

99

"More than I can say for some folks," Hack said. He was sitting in his chair again.

"The crowds aren't too bad yet," Ivy said. "I don't much like shopping when the crowds get bad."

"Me either," Hack said. "A fella ought not to leave things to the last minute."

"That's what I always say," Rhodes said.

Hack gave a dry laugh.

Rhodes was trying to think of something more to say when Lawton came into the room. "Deputy Grady needs to see you," he said in a firm, businesslike tone. Whenever he talked like that, Rhodes knew there was something wrong.

"What is it?" Rhodes said.

"I can't say," Lawton said. "She needs you in the cells."

"I guess I'd better go see, then," Rhodes said. "I'll be right back." He followed Lawton through the door.

"She's in the women's cell," Lawton said.

Rhodes walked past him, stopped to look at Swan, who was lying on his bunk with his face turned to the wall, and moved on down the corridor.

Ruth Grady was waiting for him outside the cell. "Sheriff, I think you'd better search this prisoner."

"Uh . . . what do you mean?" Rhodes was always slightly embarrassed in conversations like this. "You know I can't search a female prisoner."

"That's the problem," Ruth said.

"What? I don't understand," Rhodes said.

"I was searching the prisoner's clothing," Ruth said. "This was in the bra."

She showed Rhodes a handful of toilet paper.

"I still—"

"Betsy Higgins isn't a female prisoner," Ruth said, tossing the paper aside. "So you ought to be the one to search him."

"Oh," Rhodes said. "You mean—"

"That's right," Ruth said. "That woman in there is a man."

Chapter 12

IT TOOK A WHILE to get things sorted out and settled down. Lawton had immediately run downstairs to tell Hack, being for the first time in years one up on his friend.

"You gonna put 'em in the same cell?" Hack asked Rhodes. "Make it mighty hard on Lawton, here, to do his job."

"No, I'm not going to have them in the same cell," Rhodes said. "And before you ask, I'm not going to leave Betsy in the women's cell, either."

"Betsy?" Hack said.

"Actually his name's Barney. Short for Bernard."

"No wonder Swan didn't want to press any charges," Hack said. "Well, I guess some fellas get that way in prison." He looked at Ivy out of the corner of his eye, and Rhodes could tell that he was uncomfortable with the tone of the conversation.

Ruth had explained things to Ivy, however, and she didn't look uncomfortable at all. "People do funny things for love," she said.

101

"Like the nursing home," Ruth said, and then had to tell that story.

Rhodes was thinking while the talking was going on. No wonder Swan and Betsy—Barney—had wanted to get away. And Hack was right. No wonder Swan hadn't wanted to file any charges. In a place like Blacklin County, homosexuality and transvestitism were virtually unknown and not looked upon with favor. Anyone discovering their little secret would make things very hard on them.

Had Martin known? Was that why they were so eager to run? Rhodes would have to question them about that later, when they were more inclined to talk. Right now Swan refused to move, much less say anything, and Betsy—*Barney*—wasn't having too much to say either.

Rhodes wondered about Martin. Could he have found out something? So far there wasn't anything that Rhodes had found out about him to make the sheriff doubt that Martin would take advantage of the situation if he could and maybe engage in a little light blackmail. Or maybe a little heavy blackmail, enough to cause someone to kill him.

And that brought to mind another thought. Barney Higgins could hardly be the person to whom Mrs. Martin had referred as "that bitch." Or then again, maybe he could. It wasn't so much a matter of correctness as a matter of usage. Maybe Barney *was* "that bitch."

It was all a little too complicated, and besides there were all those presents under the tree to worry about. It was time to go home.

Rhodes went by Ivy's house and ate a cold roast sandwich while she talked about her plans for Christmas. Rhodes got more and more depressed, thinking that his plans were going to be based on everyone else's. He wondered if his daughter, Kathy, would come home. She was enjoying her teaching job, but she tried to be with her father every year at Christmas.

Then Ivy started talking about the relationship between Swan and Higgins, and between Miz White and Mr. Stuart.

Rhodes wondered if there was something in her talk that was aimed at him, but it really didn't seem that way.

"I don't see anything wrong with it," Ivy was saying. "I mean, two old people like that. What harm could there be in letting them have a room together? And what difference does it make about Mr. Swan and Mr. Higgins, really? They were just trying to have some kind of a life together."

Rhodes knew that Ivy was right, and he wondered why it was harder for him to accept one idea than the other. That was one of the things that he liked about Ivy: she put things in a perspective that helped him clarify his own thoughts and feelings. But if that was true, why couldn't he clarify his feelings about her?

Except that he knew that his feeling *were* clear. There was just something in him that kept him from acting on them, or at least from carrying his actions to their logical conclusion.

Ivy's words broke in on his thoughts. "What kind of life do you think the Martins had?"

"Not as good as they wanted people to think," Rhodes said. "They had that big house and all the gadgets that money could buy, but there was something missing. Hard to say what it was, exactly."

And maybe that was what he was afraid of, he thought. His life with Clare, before her death, had been complete. There had been trouble, sure—what life lacked trouble?— but nothing they couldn't handle together. Maybe he was afraid to try to find that kind of life again, afraid that it wouldn't be the same or that it just wouldn't work.

"She was a strange sort of woman," Ivy said.

"Who?" Rhodes asked, wondering for a second if she'd read his thoughts and was talking about Clare, who hadn't been strange at all.

"Mrs. Martin."

"You knew her?" This was something Rhodes hadn't considered.

"Only to talk to at work. They had their insurance with us. There was something about the way she looked, the way she dressed. . . ."

It occurred to Rhodes that he hadn't seen Mrs. Martin

dressed for going out of the house. "What do you mean?" he asked.

"Old-fashioned, like her hair. She dressed like someone who still loved old clothes and couldn't stand to get rid of them."

Rhodes thought about the Martins, the way the wife looked and the way the husband worked, busily accumulating money. Maybe he worked so hard because he didn't like going home. Dentists didn't get called out from home as often as doctors, so Martin had taken on the rent property as a way of escaping, of getting away. Long hours at the office, then his spare time spent on buying, furnishing, repairing.

And if you had any spare time left over . . . who would you be fooling around with?

"You think they had problems at home?" Rhodes asked.

"I don't know," Ivy answered. "Anything's possible. You can't ever really know what goes on inside a house."

Rhodes agreed, thinking of Swan and Higgins. They'd had *him* fooled, anyway. Then he told Ivy about what Mrs. Stone had overheard, and what he'd thought.

Ivy laughed. "Well, Betsy Higgins is not in the picture, unless Dr. Martin was more unusual than most people around here. It would be an awful coincidence if he were."

Rhodes agreed again. "But that doesn't leave me very much to go on," he said. "For all I know, Martin could be standing right outside the door, laughing up his sleeve at me."

"I think you ought to question his office staff," Ivy said.

"You think one of them . . ."

"I know it's a cliché," Ivy said. "Doctors and nurses, that kind of thing. But I was thinking that most women, and most men for that matter, usually fall for someone close by if they fall for anyone at all. Where would Dr. Martin meet anyone?"

"There's a word for that, isn't there?" Rhodes asked. "Starts with a *p*."

"Propinquity," Ivy said.

"That's the one," Rhodes said. And then he remembered something that had been said, the thing that had bothered

104

him a little while rolling around somewhere at the back of his mind.

He and Ivy watched part of the late movie, *Rear Window*. Rhodes drove home, wondering if Mrs. Martin had found out about her husband and chopped him up, burying him in the flowerbeds that Mrs. Stone had seen her working in. He guessed he'd have to take a look around.

The warm days were over. When Rhodes went out to feed Speedo the next morning, the temperature was close to freezing and there was a north wind that cut right through to the bone.

Speedo didn't seem to mind. In fact, he seemed to enjoy the change. He ran around the yard, occasionally stopping to pounce on an old Nike running shoe that he'd found somewhere and brought home. He grabbed the shoe and shook it violently.

"Good boy," Rhodes said. "If that were a rat, you'd break his back for sure."

Speedo tossed the shoe aside and dashed around the yard some more.

"I wish I enjoyed this as much as you do," Rhodes said. "But I don't." He poured the dry dog food into Speedo's bowl and went back into the house for a warmer coat.

When he came back out, he threw the Nike a few times so that Speedo could chase it. When they both got tired, he got in the car and drove to the jail.

It had been a quiet night. Hack had gotten a report on Phil Swan, who had served five years for armed robbery. It was the only conviction he had, and he'd been out of prison for six years now.

"If a man stays clean for that long, he might be all right," Hack said.

"Maybe," Rhodes said. "We can hold them on the assault charges for a while, though." Armed robbery wasn't too far removed from burglarizing a house and killing the occupant. "I don't guess you've had any word on anybody finding a body anywhere around."

"Not a peep," Hack said.

105

"All right," Rhodes said. "I'll check in with you later."

"You goin' shoppin'?" Hack asked, but Rhodes was already out the door.

Apartment houses, as such, were relatively new in Blacklin County. There had always been duplexes, and people had always rented out rooms, but there had never really been any demand for actual apartments.

Now there was. Rhodes wasn't quite sure why. Maybe it was because in the 1980s people just couldn't afford to buy a home, yet they preferred something a little fancier than a room in the house of some nice widow lady trying to earn a little extra money. Maybe people didn't stay in one place long enough now to put down roots. Maybe the market in real estate was so bad that no one wanted to risk buying a house that he wouldn't be able to sell later.

For whatever reason, Clearview now had apartment houses. The one in front of which Rhodes was parked had been built only a year or so earlier on one of the roads leading out of town to the south. The road wasn't well cared for, and most of the houses were old and run down, having been built fifty or sixty years earlier and passed on from owner to owner several times in the decades since. Most of them were covered in peeling paint, and the rusting hulks of thirty-year-old automobiles could be seen in more than one backyard, the weeds creeping up to window level.

The apartment house looked out of place, being new, but it was nothing fancy. Just a two-story blocky structure shaped like a squared-off U, with a narrow balcony running around the inside. There wasn't even a pool. There were sixty units, most of them occupied by singles—school teachers, workers from the cable plant, people just in town for a short while looking for a job.

Carol Shamblin lived in number 24, on the ground floor.

Rhodes knocked at the door, painted black, with cheap anodized tin numerals tacked just over the peephole. He was pretty early, but he didn't want to wait too late in the day. He had a feeling that he might have waited too long already.

He hadn't, though. After only a short wait he heard a voice saying "Who is it?"

It wasn't a particularly cordial voice. In fact, it wasn't very cordial at all. Rhodes realized that she didn't recognize him.

"Sheriff Dan Rhodes," he said.

There was a muffled noise behind the door, which Rhodes thought might have been someone saying "Oh, damn" under her breath. But he could have been mistaken.

"What do you want?"

Rhodes heard that clearly. "To talk," he said. "I want to ask you a few more questions."

The door still didn't open. "What about?"

"I'll explain when I come in," Rhodes said. He looked around the apartment house. No one was outside, and very few cars were parked beside his in the lot. Probably everyone had gone to work or was out looking for work. "It won't take long."

"I'm not dressed."

"I can wait," Rhodes said. "I don't mind."

"Oh, all right."

He heard the sound of a chain being released from its slot; then the lock of the door clicked. He turned the handle and opened the door.

Carol Shamblin walked over to the room's cheap couch and sat down. She was wearing a long maroon dressing gown. Two or three days' newspapers were scattered in front of the couch. There was a cup of coffee in a saucer sitting on the coffee table. A cigarette was balanced on the edge of a blue glass ashtray. The cigarette was half smoked and still burning. A thin edge of smoke rose from its tip.

"I didn't know you smoked," Rhodes said.

"I don't, at the office," Carol said. "It's not good for customer relations."

As Tammy had said at Dr. Martin's office, Carol was a big girl. Her white arms were thick and strong looking as they emerged from the short sleeves of the robe. Rhodes could easily imagine her helping carry the large TV set out of the office.

"I just wanted to ask you one thing," Rhodes said.

Carol picked up the cigarette and thumped it on the edge of the ashtray. "What?" she asked. She inhaled smoke and blew it out in a slow, thin plume.

Rhodes didn't mind smoke. He had once thought that he might be a failure in law enforcement because he neither smoked nor drank coffee, but since he didn't mind when others did, he'd gotten by just fine. "It's about something that Tammy said yesterday," he said.

"I'm sure you've got a point to make, Sheriff," Carol said. "But I can't quite see what it is."

"She said something about how the office would be kept open because you could clean teeth like you did when you got there yesterday."

"So?" Carol thumped the cigarette again.

"So I wanted to know what she meant by that. Just when did you get there yesterday? I don't think Tammy would have put it that way if you'd gotten there on time."

Carol leaned back on the couch. "Why didn't you ask her what she meant?"

Rhodes thought that she was much more sure of herself than she had seemed the day before. "I could have," he said. "I wanted to hear it from you, though."

"I was a little late," Carol said. She leaned forward and crushed out the cigarette. There were several other butts in the ashtray already. Maybe she was showing her nervousness in a different way today.

"How late?" Rhodes asked.

"I didn't really check. We don't punch a clock."

"I know," Rhodes said. "But you have customers with appointments. I imagine they get pretty upset when you aren't there on time."

Carol shook her short blonde hair. "Not all of them," she said.

"What time did you get in?" Rhodes didn't want to get too far from the main subject.

"About ten," she said. "I guess."

"And the office opens at nine?"

"Usually."

108

"I guess I have another question for you," Rhodes said. "Why were you so late?"

Carol searched around under a tented newspaper that lay on the floor at her feet and came out with a package of More menthol cigarettes and a green Bic lighter. She took one of the cigarettes out of the cardboard box, put it in her mouth and lit it, exhaling smoke. "You must think you know, or you wouldn't be asking," she said.

"Thinking I know isn't the same as having you tell me." Rhodes was tired of standing, looking down on Carol. He walked over to an uncomfortable brown padded chair and sat down.

"All right," Carol said. "I might as well. I was waiting for someone. He didn't show up. So I went to work."

"Someone?"

"Sammy," she said. "Dr. Martin."

Sammy? Rhodes thought. He found it hard to think of Dr. Martin as a Sammy sort of person. "Why didn't he show up?"

"I don't know." Carol leaned forward. Rhodes could see the tension in her now. "I just don't know."

"I guess you know why he was coming here, though, don't you."

"Yes, of course I do."

"Why?"

"You seem to think you know everything," Carol said. "Why don't you tell me?"

"I don't know, or I would," Rhodes said. "I have an idea, that's all."

"We were planning to go away together," Carol said. She seemed to deflate like a balloon. "He wasn't happy with his wife, and he was going to leave her."

Rhodes had heard a lot of similar stories, but he knew that the facts often proved to be different from what Carol, or anyone else hearing the story, believed. Husbands, especially husbands with thriving dental practices, didn't just leave everything behind on the spur of the moment.

"Where were you planning to go?" he asked.

"Somewhere out of state, where we could get jobs."

Oh sure, Rhodes thought, the whole thing seemed more and more unlikely. "How long had you been planning this?"

"Not long. A month, maybe."

Rhodes believed from Carol's actions the day before and from her behavior now that she was telling the truth, or what she thought was the truth. She seemed too hurt, too vulnerable, to be lying, though he might have been fooled.

"And he just didn't show up?"

Carol's cigarette went into the ashtray to join the others. "That's right. He just didn't show up." She made no attempt to keep the bitterness out of her voice.

Lost his nerve, Rhodes thought. Changed his mind. Assuming, of course, that he'd ever planned to go through with it. "Did Mrs. Martin know about the two of you?"

For the first time a shadow of evasiveness crossed Carol's face. "No," she said. "I don't think so."

Rhodes looked at her for a second. He wondered where Martin was now. Scared to face either his wife or his lover and headed for Argentina? In some cheap motel room, waiting for things to cool off? And where did this leave Higgins and Swan?

"So you just came on in to work? Gave up on him?"

"I didn't know what else to do," Carol said. "He was supposed to come by early, but he didn't. I thought . . . I thought maybe he'd be at the office. But he wasn't there, either."

No, thought Rhodes, because by then he'd been gone somewhere or other for a couple of days. Getting a head start on any pursuit?

Or had he gone back home later, attempting to reconcile things with his wife, and killed her? He could have taken a few things to make it look like a house burglary.

"I'm going to have to talk to you again, Carol," he said. "I hope you'll be around town for a while."

Carol lit another cigarette. "I'll be here. Where would I go?" She held the cigarette in front of her mouth and smiled behind it. "Who would I go with?"

It wasn't a happy smile.

Chapter 13

RHODES DROVE IDLY AROUND after his visit with Carol Shamblin, trying to sort things out in his mind. He drove through mostly residential areas, his mind registering only vaguely the many lawns decorated for Christmas with their miniature sleighs and tiny reindeer (usually not eight), their manger scenes, their shepherds watching over flocks, their characters from Peanuts decked out in scarves and mittens. He turned on his radio and even managed to ignore "White Christmas," though he did get a momentary jolt of pleasure when some disc jockey reached far enough back in his stack of oldies to find the Drifters' version of the same song.

He put what he knew together in so many ways that the patterns he came up with made a lot of sense and no sense at all. He thought of Mrs. Martin and her husband, the dentist and real estate entrepreneur. He thought of Carol Shamblin and Swan and Higgins.

He thought of buying a gift for Ivy Daniel, so he drove downtown.

* * *

When he went back by the jail, Hack eyed him carefully. "No present?" Hack asked.

Rhodes was empty handed, and confessed it.

"Well, you better look on your desk," Hack said.

Rhodes looked. There was a large coffee mug, brown on top and white on the bottom. There were two scraps of paper in it.

"Ever'body else's drawn already," Hack said. "Just you and Buddy left to go."

Rhodes reached into the mug and took one of the scraps of paper.

"Don't tell me whose name you got," Hack said. "That'd take all the fun out of it."

Rhodes unfolded the paper. The name of Ruth Grady was printed on it in block letters.

Rhodes sighed.

"Who'd you get?" Hack asked.

Rhodes looked at him. "I thought you didn't want to know."

"You could tell me," Hack said. "I wouldn't tell anybody else."

Lawton walked in from the cells just as Hack was finishing his sentence. "You'd tell," he said. "You tell everything."

"Any calls this morning?" Rhodes asked. He didn't want Hack and Lawton to get into an argument. "Anybody bite Santa Claus today?"

"Dead man lying by the highway out by the Dairy Creem. Between there and Blacklin Inn," Hack said.

"WHAT!" Rhodes yelled.

"I told you he'd act that way," Lawton said. "I told you he'd get all wrought up."

"I'M NOT—" Rhodes began. "I'm not wrought up," he said, in a more normal voice. "What about a dead man? Why didn't you—"

"See?" Lawton said. "All wrought up."

Rhodes took a deep breath and walked over to the chair at his desk. He sat down and took another breath. There was no way on earth to hurry them when they got started. It was like they'd planned it. They probably *had* planned it.

"Now," he said after a minute. "What dead man?"

"Got a call right after you left," Hack said. "Man's voice. Wouldn't say who he was. Said there was a dead man lyin' in the bar ditch out by the Dairy Creem. Then he hung up."

Rhodes wanted to ask any number of questions, but he didn't. He knew now that Hack and Lawton were teasing him along, and he wasn't going to give them any more satisfaction than he already had. He kept quiet.

"I sure don't like those anonymous phone calls," Lawton said. "They make a man wonder too much."

"Me, too," Hack said. "I hate 'em more than you do, though, because I'm the one who has to log 'em in."

"I can see how that would make you feel," Lawton said. They both looked at Rhodes. He looked back.

"I sent Buddy out to check it out," Hack said at last. "Sent an ambulance, too."

"I bet Buddy got there before that ambulance," Lawton said. "I bet a man could die of gangrene while he was waitin' for that ambulance. I remember when old man Fogarty had his heart attack—"

"Anyway," Hack said, interrupting, "I figured if it was anything important I could get you on the radio, Sheriff."

"I was questioning a suspect," Rhodes said. "A suspect in the disappearance of Dr. Samuel Martin. You may have heard of him. Local dentist? Disappeared without a trace?"

"I know about all that," Hack said.

"If it turns out that he was lying dead in the bar ditch out by the Dairy Creem," Rhodes said, "and if it turns out that I didn't hear about it, I'm going to be real depressed."

"I told you he'd act that way," Lawton said.

"I'm not acting," Rhodes said.

"I wouldn't blame you if you were," Hack said. "Not a bit. If any of my trusted employees—"

"We are trusted employees, ain't we?" Lawton asked.

Hack stared at him. Then he went on. "If any one of my trusted employees didn't inform me of somethin' of real importance, like a call about a dead man, well, I'd be depressed too."

113

Rhodes leaned back in his chair and put his feet up on the desk. "So why didn't you?" he asked.

"Didn't we what?" Hack said.

"Inform me," Rhodes said.

"I figured it wasn't worth the trouble," Hack said. "I figured that you wouldn't want to be bothered by it."

Rhodes closed his eyes. "I see," he said. "Didn't think I'd want to be bothered. Just because there's a man missing and his wife's dead, you didn't think I'd want to be bothered if somebody found a dead man in a ditch."

"That's right," Hack said. "Didn't think you'd want to be bothered."

Rhodes swung his feet to the floor and opened his eyes. "Why not?"

"Wasn't any dead man," Lawton said. His hand was on the doorknob as he began to speak, and he was out, with the door closing behind him, as soon as the last word was spoken.

Hack glared at the door. Lawton was getting too fast for him.

"Wasn't any dead man?" Rhodes said.

"That's what he said," Hack told him. "He's right, too."

"You want to explain that?"

"Well, the fella who called *said* there was a dead man, like I told you," Hack said.

"But he lied," Rhodes said. "O.K. I get it."

"Well, he didn't exactly lie," Hack said.

"What do you mean by 'exactly'?" Rhodes asked.

"Well, there was a man there, all right," Hack said.

Drunks weren't uncommon in Clearview, but they were more likely to turn up on Friday or Saturday nights. "Too much Christmas celebrating, I guess," Rhodes said.

"Not exactly," Hack said.

Rhodes was tired of the game again. He didn't say anything.

"He was passed out," Hack said. "But he wasn't drunk."

"Fainted?"

"Not exactly."

"Make it exact," Rhodes said.

"Diabetic," Hack said. "Had a flat a little piece down the road and was walkin' to a phone. Forgot to eat his mid-mornin' snack, I guess. Passed out right there in the bar ditch."

"He was walking in the ditch?" Rhodes decided to get a little of his own back.

"I didn't mean that," Hack said. "I expect he was walkin' on the shoulder of the road and fainted there. Then he prob'ly rolled down in the ditch."

"Good thing you sent the ambulance along," Rhodes said. "Buddy might have arrested him for being drunk in public."

"Buddy's the one who figured out he was diabetic," Hack said. "The fella was wearin' one of those bracelets."

"He have a name?" Rhodes asked.

"Clarence Woolfe," Hack said.

"You could've told me that to start with," Rhodes said.

"Lawton told me you'd act this way," Hack said.

Lawton was upstairs talking to Barney Higgins, who had insisted on being allowed to stay in the women's cell. Since there were no other female prisoners at the time, Rhodes hadn't seen any harm in going along with the request. Lawton had agreed.

When Rhodes walked up, Lawton said, "That sure gets off with old Hack. He can't stand for me to get to tell any part of a good story."

"He takes the calls," Rhodes said.

"I need to know what's goin' on, same as him," Lawton said.

"You're probably right, but why don't you go on down and apologize for spoiling the story. I need to talk to Barney."

"Betsy," Barney said. "Isn't that right, Mr. Lawton?"

"Whatever you say," Lawton said. "I got to go now." He walked off down the corridor, and then Rhodes heard steps going down the stairs.

Blacklin County didn't provide fancy coveralls for its prisoners like some of the larger and richer counties, but it did provide a plain white cotton jail suit similar to the ones worn

115

by convicts in the Texas Detention Center. Barney had managed to make his look almost presentable, having come up with a small piece of red ribbon from somewhere and tying it around the arm for a spot of color. It also appeared that Lawton had let him use his makeup, or at least the lipstick. There was a blush of red on his lips.

"You shouldn't stare, Sheriff," Barney said in his whiny voice. "It's not polite."

"You haven't been too polite to me yourself," Rhodes said. "Jumping me like that in the dark. Trying to run me down with that pickup truck."

"I was scared," Barney said. "Both times."

Rhodes could believe it. Barney was small and delicate, though a lot stronger than he looked. His long hair was combed around his face, and he looked so much like a woman that Rhodes still found himself thinking of Betsy instead of Barney.

"Where is the pickup, by the way?" Rhodes asked.

"There's an empty house about two blocks down," Barney said. "I parked in the backyard. I was going to get it after I got the TV set out in *my* yard."

"You were just going to take the TV and the truck and leave Phil here in jail?"

"I would've come back," Barney said. "Maybe in a couple of weeks. After you'd let him go."

Rhodes listened to the wind whine around the corners of the old jail. It wasn't easy to keep a building that old as snug as a new one, and this part wasn't nearly as comfortable as the office area. There were cracks in the walls that were hard to fill in, and various pests sometimes got in almost as easily as the wind.

"We might not let him go," Rhodes said. "Or you either."

"Moi?" Barney said.

"What?" Rhodes said.

"Me! You might not let me go?"

"That's right. We might not. I take murder pretty seriously." Rhodes meant what he said. He didn't like the idea of murder at all, the idea of someone being deprived of life.

116

He believed that everyone had a right to live, no matter if it seemed that life was treating them badly. He particularly believed that in his county. He felt in some way vaguely responsible for the lives of everyone there.

"Murder?" Higgins was yelling now in his thin, whiny voice. "Murder?"

"Hold it down, will you? I'm busy trying to write!" Phil Swan was yelling from down the corridor. He had asked for paper and pen earlier, and Lawton had given them to him. Rhodes had no idea what he was writing.

"That's enough," Rhodes said, loud enough for both of them to hear. He didn't want any communication between them right now. Obviously there hadn't been any earlier, or Swan would have told Barney the score. Probably he was still mad at Barney for running out.

"But you said murder," Barney said in a calmer tone, though not much calmer. "I thought you maybe had us on some kind of *morals* charge."

"I think you might have killed Dr. Martin's wife," Rhodes said.

"But we didn't! Surely Phil told you that! Didn't Phil tell you that? We didn't kill anybody! Sure, we saw her!" Barney was talking very fast, but now he paused. "Well, I didn't see her. And after Phil told me what he'd seen, I wasn't about to go in there. No way. Not on your life. Things like that just gross me out. We had a cat, a big black one, and it got run over. I found it in the road. Well, I just had to leave it there. Its head was all . . . well, I had to leave it. Phil had to take care of it later. We buried it in the backyard. I just couldn't touch it, even after Phil put it in a bag. We didn't kill anybody. No way."

Barney had to stop and take a breath, so Rhodes asked, "What about that cat? Part of the witchcraft thing? I wouldn't think witches would be so squeamish. Don't a lot of the rituals involve blood sacrifices?"

Barney blushed. The color in his cheeks looked natural, the same color he made them with makeup. "I'm not really a witch," he said.

"You sounded like one to me," Rhodes said. "And to Dr. Martin."

"Well, I'm not. I just do that sometimes. It's a way of . . . I don't know. Protecting myself, I guess. It works, sometimes."

"It worked on Dr. Martin," Rhodes said.

Barney smiled. "It sure did. I got our TV back."

"That's not what I mean," Rhodes said. "Nobody's seen Dr. Martin since that day you cursed him."

"Oh my God," Barney said. "You don't think that the curse . . . I mean, you can't possibly believe that I . . . why, that cat was just a cat that happened to be black . . . I didn't mean . . ."

Rhodes had a strong feeling that Barney was telling the truth, just as he had felt that Swan was. Still, the situation was too crazy for him to simply let them go. He was going to hold them in the jail for a few more days and see what turned up.

"We'll talk about it again," Rhodes said. "Is everything O.K.?"

"But you said . . . you think . . ."

"Right now I'm not sure what I think," Rhodes told him. "We'll talk later."

"Well. All right. I suppose I could use a jacket of some kind. It *is* pretty chilly in here."

Rhodes heard the wind again. "I'll have Lawton bring you another blanket," he said.

Back downstairs Rhodes told Hack that he was going to lunch. "Get Ruth Grady to go over and fingerprint the Martins' house," he said. "I know that half the people in the county have been in there, but tell her to try the kitchen and especially the areas around where the stuff was stolen. There might be something."

"I'll do it," Hack said. "You think you might find the prints of those two upstairs?"

"Maybe," Rhodes said. He wasn't sure at all. And even if the prints were found, Swan already had a story to cover himself. Barney had said he didn't go inside, but he could

118

change that if he had to. Besides, Rhodes didn't have much faith in finding any prints. He didn't recall a single case in Blacklin County ever being solved with fingerprint evidence.

"You goin' shoppin' on your lunch hour?" Hack asked.

Rhodes didn't answer.

"I may want to take a couple of hours off later in the day," Hack said. "I got a couple of presents to buy, myself."

"I'll take the calls," Rhodes said. "You can go after lunch."

"Mighty good," Hack said. "I already know what I'm gettin' for the one whose name I drew. How 'bout you?"

Rhodes still said nothing.

"Lawton was right about you," Hack said. "You're losin' your sense of humor."

"He may be right," Rhodes said, heading out the door.

Chapter 14

RHODES WAS SITTING on the Huffy Sunsprint, his feet on the pedals, staring at the speedometer. The needle of the speedometer wasn't moving, probably because Rhodes wasn't pedaling. For some reason he couldn't bring himself to try.

Maybe, he thought, if I carried the thing into the other room and put it in front of the TV set, I could do it. At least he would have something to look at besides the speedometer.

He picked up the bike and hauled it through the doorway. It really wasn't very heavy. He got it positioned without difficulty and got back on the seat.

He realized that he wasn't overly fond of bicycle seats, though this one was fairly comfortable compared to some he'd seen, skinny little things that looked almost impossible to balance on.

He put his feet on the pedals and gave a tentative push. They went right around, very fast. It seemed easy enough, so he got off and turned on the TV set. He searched through the channels for a movie, but none was on at that time of day. He had his choice of three different soap operas, a game show, some really miserable animated cartoons, and a rerun of *The Andy Griffith*

Show. He'd seen all of Andy's shows a hundred times, but he figured that it was by far the best choice.

He got back on the bike and started pedaling, meanwhile watching Barney Fife talking on the telephone to Juanita down at the diner. Barney was just beginning to sing " 'Nita, Juanita,'' when Andy walked in. By that time Rhodes's feet were flying, and the front wheel of the bike was spinning at an incredible rate, faster and faster.

It dawned on Rhodes that something was wrong. He'd thought that the exercise bike would be a painless way of getting in shape, but it wasn't supposed to be *this* easy. He looked down in front of him and saw the black knob which was used for adding resistance to the wheel. He kept pedaling as hard as he could and gradually turning the black knob to increase the resistance. When he thought he had it about right, he took his hand off the knob and turned back to the television show.

As he watched the episode unfold, Rhodes wondered if anyone had ever disappeared in Mayberry. Or if anyone had ever been murdered. He was sure that Sheriff Taylor could have solved things in less than thirty minutes and then made sure that Barney got credit for the whole thing. Rhodes wished his own case were that easy.

Then he thought about the similarity of names. Barney Fife and Barney Higgins. He remembered the episode in which Barney had dressed as a woman to fool Ernest T. Bass. There really wasn't much resemblance between him and Betsy Higgins, though. Betsy actually looked like a woman. Barney could never have fooled anyone for very long.

Rhodes's legs were getting incredibly tired. He wondered how long he'd been pedaling. A commercial came on. He hadn't begun at the beginning of the program, and this was the first commercial break. He'd been at it for ten minutes at the most. Maybe less. It seemed more like ten hours.

He stopped pedaling and got off the bike. He almost fell down. His legs felt as weak as if he'd just recovered from a three-week fever. His butt hurt where the seat had poked into it.

He took a few steps, and his legs felt better. But not a lot better. His stomach, the part of him that he worried most about, didn't feel any different at all. He could tell already that the

121

exercise program was going to be a failure. What he really needed was another bologna sandwich to go with the one he'd already eaten. He'd just started into the kitchen when the phone rang.

It was Hack. "You better get out to Sunny Dale," he said. "It's big trouble this time, and Deputy Grady is at the Martin house."

"Big trouble?" Rhodes asked.

"Food fight," Hack said.

"I'm on my way," Rhodes told him.

Sunny Dale looked perfectly calm on the outside, as if it were living up to its name. The sun was indeed shining, even though the wind pierced Rhodes's coat like a knife when he stepped out of his car. There was no one on the porch and all seemed serene.

Rhodes walked up and opened the front door; all pretense of serenity at once disappeared. He heard screaming and the crash of plastic trays hitting the walls.

A Christmas tree hung with scraggly tinsel that looked at least as old as Sunny Dale's youngest resident now stood in the entrance room. There was a moth-eaten angel on top, and the tree was covered with cloth and plastic decorations—nothing breakable. There were no lights on it. Rhodes thought it was one of the saddest-looking trees he'd ever seen. From somewhere, the speaker system probably, jolly Christmas songs were competing with the yelling. Rhodes thought he recognized "Sleigh Ride," but he wasn't sure. There was too much other noise.

He walked to the reception desk. Earlene was there, with what looked like potato salad in her hair.

"You got a gun?" Earlene asked. " 'Cause if you do I want you to shoot 'em. I'll point out which ones, and you shoot 'em."

"We wouldn't want to violate anyone's civil rights," Rhodes said.

"I would," Earlene said. "Quick."

"Where's the fight?" Rhodes asked.

"They've got Mr. Patterson trapped in—Look out!"

Rhodes turned just in time to see a man charging down the hall with a plastic bowl held over his head. There was

122

something white in the bowl, mashed potatoes, maybe, or rice. Or grits. Rhodes couldn't tell.

The old man tossed the bowl, but he didn't have any speed on it, or any accuracy. Rhodes stepped to the side and the bowl went harmlessly past him, landing somewhere behind the desk.

"Damn," Earlene said. "Now I'm going to step in that for sure."

The old man who had thrown whatever it was turned and headed back down the hall.

"He's going to Mr. Stuart's room," Earlene said. "That's where they've got Mr. Patterson hemmed up."

That was the direction from which most of the noise was coming, too, and Rhodes walked down the hall toward it. He realized now that most of what he'd thought to be yelling was really high-pitched laughter.

The speaker system was playing "Holly Jolly Christmas" by someone that sounded vaguely like Burl Ives. Rhodes tried to ignore it.

He got to Mr. Stuart's room. The door was open, and Rhodes looked in. Mr. Patterson was at bay in the far corner, his neat white outfit spattered by potatoes, gravy, and a few green peas here and there. The walls of the room looked as if they'd been repainted by one of the painters that Rhodes didn't understand. There were colorful blotches everywhere.

"Thank God you're here," Mr. Patterson said.

"What seems to be the problem?" Rhodes said, as if he couldn't see.

A man in a wheelchair had Patterson blocked in the corner. The man was holding a sectioned plate with peas and meat and gravy in their various places. He looked ready to throw it at the least provocation. Three other old men, including Mr. Stuart, sat on the bed. They were empty handed, but they were grinning as if they had helped put some of the mess on the walls. Two other men, including the one who had tossed the bowl, were standing by the bed.

"These . . . these old reprobates!" Mr. Patterson shouted. "You can just see what they've done. I want them all arrested for disorderly conduct."

"Well, now," Rhodes said. "I guess you gentlemen have a good explanation for all of this."

"Of course they don't!" Mr. Patterson said. The man in the wheelchair moved closer to him, and Mr. Patterson shut up. His face was getting very red, and Rhodes suspected that his blood pressure would set some sort of record if they could only record it.

"Mr. Stuart?" Rhodes said.

The old man slid off the bed. His legs were short, and they didn't reach the floor from the high hospital-size sleeper. He seemed pretty agile to Rhodes, at least for an eighty-seven-year-old man.

"He's keeping us apart," Mr. Stuart said. "It's not right, especially now at Christmas time."

"You and Miz White," Rhodes said.

"Yep," Mr. Stuart said.

"Of course I'm keeping them apart," Patterson said. "I've told them before—"

"I'm going to run over his foot if he don't shut up," the man in the wheelchair said. He gave Patterson a hard look.

"That's Bob Terry," Stuart said. "He'd do it, too."

"Damn right," Bob Terry said.

"Arrest them all, Sheriff," Patterson wailed. "It's lawlessness, it's anarchy, it's—"

"Just a minute, Mr. Patterson," Rhodes said. "I thought we'd agreed the last time I was out here that all this would get straightened out."

"I said we'd try something for a week and see what happened," Patterson said. "Well, I tried. But it just didn't work."

"Why not?" Rhodes asked.

"Well . . ."

"I'll tell you why not," Mr. Stuart said. "It didn't work because he didn't let it work. It was goin' just fine, but he got all upset."

"Why?" Rhodes asked.

"Because he's livin' in the fifties, that's why," Stuart said. "He ought to move into the eighties like the rest of us. I thought it was old guys like us that was supposed to live in the past, not administrators like him."

124

"I'm still not sure what you mean," Rhodes said. It was a familiar feeling for him these days.

"I mean—"

"He means that I wouldn't let him live in sin with Miz White, that's what he means!" Patterson yelled from his corner. "He means that I wouldn't permit the things *he* wants to do, even though I offered him liberal rights!"

"Liberal rights?" Rhodes asked.

"Means he'd let me sit in her room at nap time," Stuart said. "That's what he calls liberal."

The old men on the bed laughed their cracking old men's laughs.

"All right," Rhodes said. "Mr. Terry, you let Mr. Patterson go now."

Mr. Terry didn't look happy, but he moved the wheelchair. Mr. Patterson escaped his corner.

"I'll talk to them first," Rhodes said. "Then I'll talk to you."

Mr. Patterson went out into the hall, glaring back at the old men.

"Mr. Terry, you know a guy named Radford?" Rhodes asked.

"That's him," Mr. Terry said, pointing to one of the two men still sitting on the bed.

"You run over Earlene's foot in a wheelchair?" Rhodes asked him.

"Sure did," the man said. He looked sheepish. "Didn't really mean to, though."

"Well, you ought not to give Mr. Terry ideas like that," Rhodes said. "And who started all this?" He waved his arms at the walls.

"I guess I did," Mr. Stuart said. "But, Sheriff—"

"No buts," Rhodes said. "It's wrong, and I want you to clean it all up. Not Earlene. You."

The old men grumbled, but they agreed.

"And I don't want it to happen again," Rhodes said. "Or anything like it. If it does, I *will* arrest you. Or I might even have Mr. Patterson turn you out. You wouldn't want that would you, Mr. Stuart?"

"No, sir," the old man said. "I wouldn't want that. Might have to go live with my daughter."

"Everyone has to live by the laws," Rhodes said. "Sometimes we can bend them a little, but that's all. I'll talk to Mr. Patterson, but he's the boss here. He runs the show. You got that?"

The old men nodded.

"And I want you to apologize to Earlene," Rhodes said. There was more grumbling, and then the nods.

"All right," Rhodes said. He went out and left them there.

Patterson was at the reception desk. He'd cleaned his whites a bit, and Earlene had the mess out of her hair.

Rhodes glanced down the hall to the women's wing. A white head slipped back inside a doorway.

"Well?" Mr. Patterson asked.

"Well, it won't happen again," Rhodes said. "At least, I don't think it will."

"What about punishing them?" Patterson asked.

"They aren't kids," Rhodes said. "They know they were wrong, and they'll clean up their mess. I'm sure not going to arrest them."

"I guess I didn't really expect that," Patterson said.

Earlene looked disappointed.

"I think you ought to rethink your rules," Rhodes said. "I don't like to tell a man how to run his business, but it seems to me I see in the papers all the time about old people meeting in places like this and getting married."

"Not in 'places like this,' " Patterson said. "Sunny Dale is different. At Sunny Dale, we don't allow—"

"Don't allow old people to fall in love?"

"I wouldn't put it that way," Patterson said.

"Well, you might at least think about it," Rhodes said. "It's Christmas, and a lot of the families will be coming in regularly. You could ask some of them how they'd like to have married couples living here and see if they'd object."

"Well . . ."

"And if any of them objected, you could bring Mr. Stuart to them and let him hear. Then maybe he'd understand and give in a little bit."

"I suppose it's possible," Patterson said. "But I don't like to think that the inmates are running the asylum."

"You probably didn't mean to say that."

Patterson thought about it. "I guess I didn't. Not exactly the way I said it, at least."

"Besides," Rhodes said, "you wouldn't want any families or friends to walk into something like this mess today."

"That's true too," Patterson said. "It's just that it's so hard to know what to do. I try to do the right thing . . ."

"I'm sure you do," Rhodes said, "and I'm sure you do a fine job."

"Thanks, Sheriff," Patterson said. "I think sometimes that no one really cares. They just dump these old people here and leave it up to me to cope with them. As you can see, most of them are perfectly capable of taking care of themselves, at least for short periods of time. I don't mean to cause you trouble, and I know you have other things to do, but these last few weeks have been a real strain on me. This romance business is for the birds."

"I know what you mean," Rhodes said.

"Does this mean you aren't going to shoot anybody?" Earlene said.

"I don't think I'll have to," Rhodes said.

"You don't know this bunch very well," Earlene said. "You just wait till you're out the door."

"They'll behave," Rhodes told her. "I'll bet that if you go down there right now, they might even apologize to you."

"Sure they will," Earlene said.

"Give it a try, Earlene," Mr. Patterson said. "It couldn't hurt."

"If one of 'em runs over my foot with that wheelchair, I'm suing you and this whole place," Earlene said.

Mr. Patterson looked pained.

"Don't worry," Rhodes said. "It won't happen."

"I hope not," Patterson said. "She's not kidding."

"I believed her," Rhodes said. As he went out through the entrance hall, "Silver Bells" wafted to his ears through the speaker system. He managed to get out before he heard more than a line or two.

127

Chapter 15

RHODES DROVE OUT to the Martin house, where Ruth Grady was finishing up with her fingerprinting.

"I raised plenty of prints," she told him. "All you have to do is match them up."

"Most of them are the Martins', I'm sure," Rhodes said. "Did you find anything else interesting?"

"I looked over the whole place pretty carefully," she said. "I didn't find a thing."

She meant that she hadn't found a thing that would be of help. There were plenty of things to find, otherwise. Rhodes sent her back to the jail with her prints while he sat down at the kitchen table and thought. Surely there was something. . . .

He went back out into the garage, which was really more like a carport since it didn't have any doors. He admired the '57 Chevy for a minute and then looked around. The usual tools that he might have expected to find were missing, but because Martin was a sort of handyman who liked to fix up his own property, rental and otherwise, there was a storage shed out back for the tools.

Except for one long wooden box with triangular ends joined by a wooden bar. It sat near the back door and contained two hammers, some nails, several screwdrivers, a pair of Vise Grips, a socket set, several plastic packages of screws, two pairs of pliers, and some wire. Probably the box Martin grabbed up when he had a quick repair to make. He wouldn't want to carry tools around in his Suburban.

Rhodes wondered about a crowbar. Probably there should have been a short crowbar in the box, but there wasn't one. That didn't necessarily mean anything. It *could* mean that Mrs. Martin's killer had grabbed up a handy weapon, but it didn't have to mean that. And even if it did, Rhodes didn't see how that helped him.

He got in his car and drove back to the jail.

"No presents?" Hack asked.

"No," Rhodes said. "No presents."

"How about my time off?"

"Go ahead," Rhodes said.

Hack got up. "I know what I'm gonna get," he said. "Already got it figured out."

He put on a coat that had been hanging on the back of his chair. "Just takes a little thought, is all. You oughta give it some thought, Sheriff."

"I will," Rhodes said.

"I'll be back in a little while," Hack said.

Rhodes sat down by the radio and phone. "Take your time," he said.

Hack was gone for less than an hour. He came back in with a bright package wrapped in red foil and tied with a green ribbon. "Don't look," he said. "You'll know what this is and who got it."

"It would be hard to avoid," Rhodes said.

"I think it's pretty," Hack said, putting it under the tree. "We get any calls?"

"Just one," Rhodes said.

"Yeah? Who was it?"

"Didn't say," Rhodes told him.

"Didn't say?"

129

"Anonymous call."

"Oh," Hack said. "Wouldn't give you a name?"

"Right."

Hack looked at the presents under the tree. "Man or woman?"

"Man," Rhodes said.

Hack walked over to the tree and picked up a small package with a card on it. "This 'un's for me," he said. He shook the package near his ear, but it didn't appear to make a sound. All Rhodes could hear was the rattle of paper in Hack's hand.

"Say what he wanted?" Hack asked after he put the package back down.

"Yes," Rhodes said. He got up from Hack's chair and went to his own desk. Hack walked over and sat in his chair.

"Well," Hack said. "What did he want?"

"Report somebody being murdered," Rhodes said. He busied himself with some papers on his desk, shuffling through them and then stacking them.

"Murder?" Hack asked.

"That's what he said." Rhodes set the stack of papers aside and reached to the back of the desk for another bunch. He started shuffling through them.

"All right, dang it," Hack said. "I give up. Lawton said you'd been touchy lately, and I said no. But I'm beginnin' to think he was right, for once."

Rhodes put down the papers and looked over at Hack. "Why do you say that?"

"It's not like you to try to get back at a fella, that's why." Hack shucked off his coat and hung it on the back of his chair.

Rhodes smiled. "Get back at a fella for what?"

"Nothin'," Hack said.

Rhodes smiled wider. "Seems to me that you're the one who's getting touchy," he said. "Since there's no reason for me to get back at you."

"All right, I get it. You don't have to rub it in."

"Rub what in?"

"Never mind," Hack said. "You don't want to tell me, you don't have to."

130

"Tell you what?"

"Who got murdered. Where they was when it happened. Who you sent out there. And why you're sittin' so calm about it all."

"I didn't say anybody was murdered."

"You said—"

"I said that the caller wanted to *report* a murder," Rhodes said.

"Oh," Hack said.

"There's a big difference," Rhodes said. "Like the difference between a dead body in a ditch and a man with diabetes in a ditch."

"I said I got it," Hack said. "I swear you're just as bad as Lawton said you was."

"I guess you're right," Rhodes said.

"I know I am. But you better tell me anyway," Hack said.

The game had gone on long enough, but Rhodes had enjoyed it. It didn't begin to make up for the times Hack had teased him with the details of a call, but it was a start.

"Well," Rhodes said, "a man called to report a murder on Apple Street. Said it sounded like someone was being killed out behind a garage. Since I was stuck here, I called Buddy to check it out."

"What'd he find?"

"He found out that some people just don't have very well developed musical tastes. Or maybe they do. Maybe they're *too* developed."

"Music?"

"Larry Tilley, Lester Tilley's son," Rhodes said. "Has him a little heavy metal band. Call themselves the Manglers. They play on weekends at some of the clubs around, if the clubs can't get anybody else. They were rehearsing after school in Lester's garage. I guess if you were a little hard of hearing you might take it for the sound of somebody getting killed. Buddy says that Larry can scream the high notes so you'd think so. I'm going to take his word for it."

"They wear those spiky leather gloves and stuff?" Hack asked.

"I guess," Rhodes said. "You a heavy metal fan?"

131

"I lean more toward Eddy Arnold," Hack said. "But I know about stuff like that."

Rhodes thought about Mr. Stuart. "An eighties kind of guy, huh?"

"I wouldn't say that, but I sort of keep up," Hack said.

Rhodes thought of asking how, but he didn't. He wasn't sure he wanted to know.

That night Rhodes was talking about Dr. Martin to Ivy. He liked to discuss cases with her because she had a lot of common sense, and she sometimes saw things he missed.

"You ought to sit down and go over everything from the beginning," she said. "It would be a lot easier if Dr. Martin would turn up."

"I don't think there's much chance of that," Rhodes said.

"Then let's look at it logically."

They were sitting on the couch in Ivy's living room, watching the ten o'clock news. Child abuse, trouble in Nicaragua, a terrorist incident in the Middle East. Nothing new.

"It's not easy to be logical when we're sitting like this," Rhodes said. It was sitting close to Ivy that had gotten him engaged. Sitting close and what came next.

Ivy laughed and pushed him away, moving to a safer cushion. "Who would want him to disappear?" she asked.

"Nobody," Rhodes said. "Maybe his wife, but now she's dead."

"But his renters didn't like him?"

"Some of them didn't."

"And you've got two of them in jail."

Rhodes thought about it. "Yes, but I'm pretty sure they didn't do anything to him. I think they wanted to be left alone. The cursing and all that about the TV set was a mistake."

Ivy looked at him. "But they might have killed Mrs. Martin."

"Why?" Rhodes said. "For a VCR and a TV set? They already had a TV set."

"Maybe she knew something."

"What? That they were homosexual? I don't think they would have killed her for that. Who would she have told?"

"I can see you've been thinking about all this before," Ivy said.

"I guess so," Rhodes told her. He hadn't even realized that he'd been thinking, though, so he didn't feel he deserved much credit. "So who does that leave?"

"The hygienist," Ivy said. "That Carol Shamblin."

Rhodes shifted on the couch, trying to get comfortable. The tops of his legs above the knees were very sore. The bicycle must do some good if it made you that sore.

"Why do you say it that way?" Rhodes asked.

"What way?"

"That way. I don't know how to describe it."

"I guess I just don't like women who plan to run away with someone else's husband," Ivy said.

"I wonder if Martin ever really planned anything like that," Rhodes said. "I wonder if he could possibly have meant it, even if he said it."

"It doesn't seem likely," Ivy said, shaking her head.

"He may have staged the whole thing," Rhodes said. "Then sneaked back and killed his wife. If there was a crowbar in the garage, he'd know about it." He explained to Ivy about the tool box.

"But the missing television set doesn't fit," Ivy said. "A fugitive wouldn't take a TV set."

"He would to throw us off," Rhodes said. "He might have taken a few things, ditched them, and left. The whole house was set up to look as if there'd been a burglary, but it's hard to tell if anything's really missing, except for the big stuff. Whoever did it might have taken just a few things, hoping we'd think more things were missing."

"Was Dr. Martin that smart?"

"I don't know," Rhodes said. "I guess a dentist has to be pretty smart to get out of school."

"Say it wasn't Martin. Who does that leave you with?"

"Hardly anybody," Rhodes said. "There's Little Barnes, but I don't know how we'd ever get him to admit it. What we

133

need is a body. Or for Martin to turn up wandering around the back roads with a severe case of amnesia."

"Does that ever happen in real life?" Ivy asked. "Or just on the soap operas?"

"I don't know," Rhodes said. "I never heard of a real case of it, though."

"So you're in real trouble on this one, right?"

"Right."

"At least it's not an election year."

"Sure it is," Rhodes said. "I've already been elected."

"So now you get to enforce the law."

"I guess so, but it would be a lot easier if I could find someone to enforce it on."

Ivy got off the couch and turned off the TV set. "I'm not in the mood for *Nightline*," she said.

Rhodes was going to ask if there weren't some old movie on, but then he thought better of it. Ivy didn't necessarily share his enthusiasm for obscure Hollywood classics.

Ivy sat back on the couch closer to Rhodes than she had been. He put his arm around her shoulders.

He knew that he was going to wind up remembering only too well why he was unofficially engaged.

Chapter 16

THE NEXT DAY Rhodes woke up *officially* engaged. He had admitted to himself and to Ivy that their romance had reached a serious stage. They had set the date.

Rhodes didn't want to tell anyone yet, however. He wanted Kathy to be the first to know, and he wanted to tell her in person when she came home for Christmas.

If she came. He still hadn't heard from her.

Ivy understood. "We're both too old to worry about the formalities," she said.

"Me, maybe," Rhodes said. "Not you."

Ivy laughed. "I didn't get these gray hairs from worrying," she said.

Now that he was entirely committed, Rhodes felt better about the whole thing. In fact, he wondered why he had ever hesitated. It had been foolish and even childish.

But he still hadn't bought any Christmas presents.

He went out to feed Speedo, who didn't want to come out of the barrel. It had gotten even colder, though the wind was not blowing so hard. The sun was shining and glinting on the frost that topped the grass in the yard, the grass that

Rhodes had intended to mow one more time before it got really cold. He'd never gotten around to it, so the lawn was a little shaggy. Well, he could mow it early in the spring.

There was nothing new at the jail. Hack had logged in a few drunks and there had been a robbery at the Dairy Creem. The robber had waved around some kind of gun and demanded three cheeseburgers and three large orders of fries. The frightened clerks had complied.

"I called the hospital emergency room," Hack said, "but nobody had checked in with stomach cramps. I guess he got off clean."

"Their cheeseburgers aren't that bad," Rhodes said.

"Lawton ate one there last month, and he says they are," Hack said.

"How are the prisoners?"

"Both doin' fine. That Swan writes a lot. Must be writin' letters to his momma."

"I can't see any way to tie them into this Martin case," Rhodes said. "I think I'll release them."

"What if it turns out they're in it?"

"I'll tell them to stay in town," Rhodes said.

Hack looked doubtful, but he said, "I'll call the judge for you."

The day went by without anything of interest occurring. The radio crackled occasionally, but everything was routine. Rhodes caught up on his paperwork and worried what he'd say at the next Commissioners' Court meeting. The commissioners tended to get a little touchy if there were any unsolved murders in the county. Of course no one was really sure that Dr. Martin had been murdered, not that an unsolved disappearance was much better. And there wasn't any doubt about Mrs. Martin.

He went out and got hamburgers for lunch from the Dairy Creem. Hack admitted that his was just fine. "Just the right amount of grease on the wrapper," he said. "It was prob'ly the cheese that made Lawton sick. A man oughtn't to eat cheese with meat."

Rhodes, who liked cheeseburgers, didn't say anything to that.

Late in the afternoon Rhodes said, "I'm going to take off now. I think everything's under control here, and I've finally got caught up on all the papers. You and Lawton need anything?"

"Lawton can get us supper," Hack said. "I don't want anything yet, and you need to go shoppin'."

Rhodes went outside into the late afternoon cold. He could tell that by night the temperature would dip even lower than the night before. It was getting to be wintertime. The air made the inside of his nose cold when he breathed in, and he thought he could smell leaves burning somewhere. There was an ordinance against burning, but he wasn't going to hunt for the offender. It was too late in the day, and besides he liked the smell.

The metal door handle of the car was cold under his hand, and he wondered if he should buy himself some gloves. He'd had a pair that he liked and had worn them for years—genuine leather, lined with soft rabbit fur—but they'd finally worn out and he hadn't bought any more. He thought he'd just drive down to Hubbard's and look for a pair, maybe see if anybody had bitten Santa lately.

Hubbard's closed at five-thirty, so he had a few minutes to spare if he could find a parking place. He did, only a block away. He got out of the car and was up on the sidewalk about to go in Hubbard's when he saw a familiar figure down the street by Lee's Drug Store. Little Barnes had just gotten out of his dark blue pickup and started for Lee's.

Something that had been nagging at the back of Rhodes's mind pushed its way to the front, and instead of going in Hubbard's he walked down the street toward Lee's. When he came up in front of it, he looked through the long plate-glass window and saw Little Barnes all the way at the back of the store, talking to Billy Lee, the pharmacist. Probably Little had caught a winter cold and was asking for a recommendation and a remedy. He'd gone to the right man, because Billy Lee knew his business.

Rhodes stepped off the sidewalk and looked into the

pickup. The windows were rolled up, of course, thanks to the cold weather, but there was really nothing to see. Like a lot of people in Blacklin County, Little had a gunrack in the back window, but there were no guns in it. Theft was too much of a problem.

Rhodes didn't try the doors. He would wait and talk to Little when he came out. There were still shoppers on the streets and in the stores, but on the whole the street was better.

Rhodes stood by the truck and spoke to some of the pass-ersby. If anyone wondered what he was doing there, no one asked. He knew many of them by sight if not by name, just as they knew him, but he knew none of them very well. Most of them probably thought he was standing by his own pickup.

Little's truck was not immaculately clean, but it wasn't particularly dirty, either. There were mud spots on it, and there was a lot of mud stuck up under the back wheel wells. The truck hadn't been washed very recently.

Rhodes stepped back and looked in the pickup's bed. There was an accumulation of hay next to the cab and a couple of strands of baling wire, but that was all.

Except that the floor looked a little gritty. Rhodes ran his hand over the floor, then looked at his fingers. He rubbed the tips together. Cement. He'd seen Little Barnes digging the postholes, and he recalled seeing the bags of cement stacked against the pickup that day. Barnes had said he was going to set his fence posts in concrete.

Rhodes shivered, and he wondered if it was because of the cold. It was getting dark now, and the streetlights had come on, along with the Christmas lights. People were leaving the stores, getting in their cars, and heading for home. He could hear the cars starting, smell the exhaust.

Martin had disappeared, and Rhodes had thought it was as if he'd fallen down a well. A well like the one he'd seen the day he visited Little Barnes. The one he'd asked about drinking the water from.

Rhodes stood there in the street in the cold, feeling it creep into his coat and past his shirt. But he thought that Dr. Martin

138

was probably colder, down in the bottom of that well in the water, his feet encased in cement.

He could be wrong, though. It was just a thought, based on Martin's ability to bring out the worst in people and Little Barnes's known habits. That, and the fact that the well was there, the cement was there, and Dr. Martin had been there. It was possible.

Rhodes looked up and saw Little Barnes come out of the drug store door. He was holding a white paper sack in one hand and wearing what looked like exactly the same pair of Big Mac overalls and the same red and black flannel shirt that he had worn the other day. The sleeves of the shirt were still rolled up. Evidently the cold didn't bother Little all that much.

Barnes didn't see Rhodes until he stepped down off the curb. He didn't look pleased to see the sheriff standing by his pickup, but then he didn't often look pleased at anything.

"Hello, Little," Rhodes said. "Just looking over your truck."

"Find what you were lookin' for?" Barnes asked.

"Don't know," Rhodes said. "I wanted to talk to you again about Dr. Martin."

Barnes set the white bag down carefully on the hood of the pickup. "What about him?"

Rhodes gestured to the pickup bed. "I see you've been mixing cement. You had some out there at your place the day I was talking to you, the day after Martin—"

Barnes's fist hit Rhodes in the chest like a concrete block. He wouldn't have thought such a big man could move so fast. Rhodes went backward for three steps, then sat down in the street. Hard. The headlights from a car hit him, and the car swerved to get by. Rhodes scrambled to his knees and got out of the way.

When he looked up, he saw that Little Barnes had the pickup door open and was reaching in behind the seat. As Rhodes got to his feet, Little came out with a .22 automatic rifle in his hands.

"Put that thing back, Little," Rhodes said. "Somebody might get hurt." A .22 was not very powerful, and Barnes

139

probably carried it to shoot at turtles in his stock tank. But a slug in the right spot—say the eye or the nose—could kill you as quick as a slug from a .44.

Barnes ignored Rhodes's voice. He hopped up on the sidewalk, pointed the gun at Rhodes, and pulled the trigger.

Rhodes felt the tug of the fabric at the right shoulder of his coat at almost the same time he heard the shot. Then he smelled the powder.

Barnes was off and running down the street, carrying the rifle.

Rhodes looked over his shoulder. The slug had no doubt gone right through the window of the furniture store across the street, but there didn't seem to be anyone shopping there. Rhodes hoped the slug was now resting safely in a sofa cushion. He got to the sidewalk and started off after Barnes.

Billy Lee put his head out the door of the drug store as Rhodes passed.

"Call the jail," Rhodes told him. "Have them send a deputy." As he ran he was working the snap of the holster. He hated to take the pistol out on the streets, but he was afraid he might need it. He knew that he wouldn't fire, however, unless he had an absolutely clear shot.

Ahead of him Little Barnes ran along the sidewalk, past a jewelry store, a gift shop, and an appliance store. A woman and a small boy were coming out the door of the latter, and Barnes bowled them over. The boy was crying when Rhodes passed, but he seemed all right. The mother was hugging him. Rhodes didn't stop to check on them.

Barnes kept on going, past the funeral home, the variety store, and another furniture store. In the next block there was a Western Auto store and a car repair garage. Rhodes was likely to be able to get in a clear shot, and he took the pistol out of the holster. He knew that he wasn't likely to hit Barnes, even as big as he was, but maybe he could slow him down just by firing.

They had been running for only two blocks, but Rhodes was getting winded. He thought about the exercise bike and wondered if he should have spent more time on it. Maybe next week, if he got out of this one, he would get started.

His only consolation was that Little Barnes seemed to be slowing as well.

Barnes passed the garage and almost got run over by a red Yugo driven by Miss Landers, the librarian. She had gotten it in Dallas; it was the only Yugo in town. Rhodes had been about to risk a shot, but he was afraid of hitting Miss Landers. Or worse, her Yugo. She had to take special care of it, since no one in the county would work on it.

The red of Miss Landers's taillights reflected off Barnes's Big Macs as she passed safely by. Barnes went on across the street, and Rhodes realized that not only was it getting darker but that Barnes was getting beyond the best of the street-lights. In town the Christmas lights and store lights had made vision easier. Now Barnes was passing an abandoned building that had housed, in Rhodes's memory, a cleaning firm, a garage, and a garment factory. There were lights only on the corners now, and Barnes was becoming a black blur.

Rhodes tried to speed up, and he found that he could go only a little faster; he didn't gain much. In a few seconds Barnes would be at the Presbyterian church. Rhodes hoped that the Reverend Funk had already gone home.

When Barnes reached the church, he stopped. Rhodes thought he could see his shoulders heave as Barnes tried to get a deep breath. Barnes was standing in front of the church's manger scene, which had been used each year for a generation or two. It featured life-sized figures of the three wise men, two shepherds, Joseph, Mary, and assorted animals. Rhodes had never looked inside the wooden manger, but he supposed that there was a life-sized baby Jesus in it. The figures were all heavy, made of chalky material like that of thousands of cats, dogs, and parrots sold at roadside stands throughout the South. Through the years the figures had been treated with loving care, repainted when the old paint wore thin, and generally become a traditional part of Clearview's Christmas scene. When parents bundled their children in the car to drive around the town and look at decorations, no trip that failed to pass by the Presbyterian church for a look at the manger scene was considered complete. Other churches

141

had tried to compete, without much success, by using living figures. Rhodes was glad there were no living figures here.

Barnes had caught his breath and was looking back over his shoulder. He saw Rhodes pounding along after him, ran between two wise men, and ducked behind the crude wooden shelter that housed the manger. Rhodes could see him quite well, thanks to the spotlights that were used to make the scene visible to passersby.

Then Rhodes heard the crack of the .22. The light shining toward Barnes shattered in a crackle of glass and went dark.

There was another crack. This time Rhodes didn't feel the tug of the bullet, so he knew that it had passed him completely by. He hoped that it had passed everything safely by. He seemed to remember from somewhere in his reading that a .22 slug could travel for more than a mile, though it wouldn't have much power at the end of its trip.

Rhodes dropped to his stomach, his blood pounding in his ears, his breath rasping in his throat. He took in several gulps of the cold air, breathing deeply to try to relax. Then he tried to focus his eyes on the manger scene.

He saw what looked like a darker shadow within the shadows, and he thought it might be Little Barnes, kneeling for another shot.

Rhodes steadied his pistol with both hands and fired.

There was a thudding sound, and one of the wise men's heads fell off. It was the black wise man who was hit.

Balthazar?

Rhodes couldn't remember, though he'd seen *Ben Hur* five or six times. The only name that came to mind was Messala, the only good role that Stephen Boyd had ever had. And Messala hadn't been one of the wise men.

There was an answering crack from the .22, and the slug dug up dirt ten feet in front of Rhodes and twenty feet to the left. Barnes couldn't see him very well, either.

Another slug followed, whining off the sidewalk. That one was much closer, and Rhodes had seen the spark when the lead hit the walk.

"Who's shooting at us?"

Rhodes didn't jump at the voice at his back, but that was

only because he was lying flat on his belly and couldn't jump. He'd been so wrapped up in his chase and in Little's firing that he hadn't heard Ruth Grady come up. In fact, he'd completely forgotten that he'd asked Billy Lee to make the call to the jail.

"Little Barnes," he said after recovering a bit.

Ruth was lying beside him now, not too close. "Why?"

"I'm not sure," Rhodes said. "I stopped to ask him a few more questions about Dr. Martin, and he took off."

"Didn't sound like he had a very powerful gun," Ruth said.

"He doesn't. A twenty-two rifle. He could still hurt somebody, though."

At that minute Barnes fired two more shots. Rhodes could have sworn that he heard one of them pass by his ear, but he was probably imagining it.

"We need to get up a barricade around the area," Ruth said. "Keep the citizens out of harm's way."

"Good idea," Rhodes said. "I don't think he has many shots left, though. We might be able to get him when he runs out."

"How many?"

"How many left?" Rhodes tried to remember. "He's fired seven or eight times. I think."

"But we don't know how many the magazine holds or whether it was full to begin with," Ruth said.

"Or whether it was loaded with shorts, longs, or long rifles," Rhodes said. "So he might have two or six or even none."

He looked around. Most of the houses nearby had on lights, and he hoped that whoever was in them had enough sense to stay in them. The shots had no doubt been heard; he hoped that no one got too curious.

"So what do you think?" Ruth asked.

"About the barricade? I still think it's a good idea; I just don't know how soon we could get one up, or whether we'd be in time. I don't know what we'd do about the people in these houses."

A car was coming down the street. Rhodes hoped that he and Ruth were far enough to the side so that its lights wouldn't

143

sweep over them. He also hoped that Little Barnes wouldn't take a notion to shoot at whoever was in the car just for spite.

The lights passed them by, and there was no shot. The driver of the car went blissfully on his or her way, unaware of what was going on just a few feet off to the side of the street.

"I'll tell you what," Rhodes said. "Now that there're two of us, let's try to surround him. If that doesn't work, you get in touch with Hack, get him to call Buddy, and start on the barricade."

"Surround him?"

"Wrong phrase. I thought you might try to draw him off, get him to fire a round or two, while I sneak up behind him." Rhodes thought about what Randolph Scott might do. "I'll try to get the drop on him."

"I guess we could try." Ruth sounded doubtful.

Rhodes began to inch himself backward. "When I get far enough away, I'll call you. He's behind the stable. Shoot that way."

"All right," Ruth said.

When Rhodes had gotten past Ruth's feet, he rolled over and over into the darkness. Then he got to his knees and crawled. Finally he arrived at some kind of bush that he couldn't identify in the dark. "O.K.," he said.

Ruth got off two shots from her Police Special in rapid succession. One of the rounds thunked into the stable. The other shot off the hand of one of the shepherds, the hand holding the shepherd's crook. Rhodes shook his head as he ran. The Reverend Funk wasn't going to be easy to pacify. Rhodes might have to remind him about who had helped him shovel off the parking lot when Mr. Clawson's cows got loose and wandered onto it.

Ruth fired again and shot the frankincense out of the hands of one of the wise men, or maybe it was the myrrh. At least that wise man still had his head.

Barnes didn't fire back. Rhodes took that to mean that he was either out of cartridges or very low.

Rhodes was making a wide circle around the church building, a very old red brick structure that looked more like a

144

very large Tudor house than a church. He passed around behind it and out of sight of the manger scene.

The other side of the church was fairly well lit, since a streetlight was on the corner and there were no bushes or trees to obstruct its beam. This part of the block was the church parking lot. Rhodes got up on his toes and ran as quiety as he could on the asphalt.

He was exposed when he came around the next corner at the front of the church, but no one was there. Barnes was still hiding behind the stable, in the darkness of the shadow cast by the church on the one side and the stable on the other. Rhodes knew he would have to be careful making the next turn.

Ruth Grady had no way of knowing where he was, but she must have suspected that he was still circling the building. He heard her fire two more shots. One of them was followed by the sound of glass breaking.

Rhodes thought about the stained-glass windows in the church building. He supposed that they were very old and probably valuable. Maybe only a small corner of one was smashed.

With his pistol ready, he edged his way to the corner of the building. He risked a look around it and saw what he thought was Barnes, a hulking shadow within the shadows behind the stable.

He couldn't tell which way Barnes was looking or what he was doing. It was possible that he had been carrying some more .22 rounds in one of the pockets of his overalls and that he was reloading, but it didn't seem very likely. More probably he was just crouched there trying to decide what to do, whether to give himself up or make a run for it, whether to fire a few more shots and make things worse for himself or call it quits before someone got seriously hurt.

Rhodes eased around the corner of the building, the rough brick pulling at the fabric of his coat. He was going to have to step out from the wall because it was lined with small, low bushes with sticky leaves. Several of them pushed their way through his pants and pricked his legs.

Rhodes realized that he was sweating in spite of the cold.

He held his pistol in his left hand and wiped his right on his pants leg. Then he changed hands and wiped his left. He didn't blame himself for being just a little bit nervous. He hadn't had to shoot anyone in a long time.

He didn't think he'd have to shoot Barnes, either, now that he had the drop on him.

Just like Randolph Scott.

All he had to do was get close enough to Barnes to make it clear that Little had no chance, then announce his presence. That would be that.

Or so Rhodes had hoped.

He stepped out onto the narrow sidewalk that ran alongside the bushes and made his way closer to the dark bulk of Barnes, his feet not making a sound on the walk.

When he was about fifteen feet away, he guessed he was close enough. "All right, Barnes," he said, leveling his pistol. "Drop the rifle. I've got you covered."

Before he even had time to wonder how many times he'd heard Audie Murphy say those lines, the church building fell on him.

Chapter 17

IT WASN'T THE CHURCH BUILDING, but it might as well have been. It was Little Barnes, as Rhodes realized when he came to while Barnes was dragging him over the threshold of the church door. Barnes could probably have carried him, but he needed one hand to hold the .22 and Rhodes's pistol.

There were no lights on in the church building, and Rhodes could see only the dim shapes of the rows of pews, the altar rail, and the pulpit when Barnes let go of him. Rhodes was lying on the narrow strip of carpet between the two banks of pews, and Barnes was standing over him.

Rhodes thought of saying something like, "You'll never get away with this," but he thought better of it.

Barnes was walking toward the altar when Rhodes sat up and rubbed his head. He didn't know what Barnes had hit him with, but it had been hard. There was a knot on the left side of Rhodes's head, and when he touched it a streak of pain went through his skull as if someone had driven a knife in it.

147

He must have groaned, because Barnes walked back to him. "You and me need to get out of here," Barnes said.

Rhodes wondered if Ruth Grady had any idea of what had happened or if she was still waiting for him to do something. He didn't say anything to Barnes. His head hurt too bad.

"Or we could stay for a while," Barnes said. "Don't matter much to me. You decide."

Rhodes still didn't say anything.

Barnes casually pointed the pistol at Rhodes. "I said, 'You decide.' "

Rhodes decided.

He threw himself at Barnes's legs. The fact that he was sitting down made it hard to get any momentum, but he had enough to throw Barnes off balance. By grabbing at one of Barnes's ankles, he managed to topple him.

As Barnes fell the pistol went off. Rhodes heard the tinkling of glass as the bullet passed through one of the chandeliers. He wondered if a gun had ever been fired in a church before, but he didn't have much time to think about it.

Barnes was cursing and trying to sit up, and Rhodes was trying to get on top of him and prevent it. Rhodes was also trying to get his hands on his pistol; he seemed to lose it too often.

There was very little room to struggle in the aisle of the church. Rhodes could feel Barnes's breath on his face as the big man twitched under him, and then he could feel himself being slowly twisted to the side against the edge of the pews. He knew that Barnes could crush the breath out of him with very little effort.

Then his hands grasped the pistol in Barnes's fingers. He got both hands on it and pulled as hard as he could. It fired again, the sound nearly deafening him. This time the slug thunked into the wall at the other end of the pew row.

Maybe I'll get a single action next time, Rhodes thought.

The pistol came free in his hands. His head was hurting, and Barnes was mashing him against the pews. He couldn't remember how many times the pistol had been fired. He couldn't remember where Barnes's rifle was, or even when he'd seen it last. He was blacking out.

Then there was another shot.

This one twanged into one of the organ pipes at the front of the church. Rhodes groaned again, not just from the pain in his head.

"Freeze, scumbag!" Ruth Grady yelled.

" 'Scumbag'?" Rhodes said, or thought. Even Ruth had been watching too much TV.

Barnes didn't freeze. He slithered away from Rhodes down the pew row like a python after a big meal.

Rhodes started after him, his head pounding.

Barnes reached the end of the row and turned into the aisle. Rhodes crawled faster and threw himself at Barnes's legs.

Barnes fell, and they rolled together in the narrow aisle. As Barnes rolled on top of him, Rhodes felt his elbows getting rug burns through his shirt sleeves. His jacket sleeves had been pushed up almost to his shoulders in the struggles.

Barnes was grunting and Rhodes was groaning. Then Rhodes felt Barnes's body thumping into him, as if someone else had joined the fight.

Someone had. Ruth Grady was kicking and pummeling Barnes.

"Get up!" she yelled. "Get up, or I'll fire!"

Rhodes felt the weight suddenly leave him, and Barnes rolled off and stood up. Rhodes saw him standing over him in the dim light that came through the stained-glass windows, red and green colors falling across his face.

Barnes towered over the much shorter Ruth Grady, and Rhodes tried to sit up, to tell her that she was standing too close to Barnes. He didn't manage to do either, because Barnes thought of it first. He reached out and grabbed Ruth's wrist, twisting the gun to the side.

He was going to hit her when Rhodes tackled him again.

Barnes didn't let go of Ruth's wrists, and this time all three of them were piled in the aisle.

Rhodes was in the middle, feeling like the meat in a strange sandwich.

Ruth Grady was on one side, kicking and scratching with her free hand, getting Rhodes as often as Barnes.

149

Barnes was on the bottom, heaving upward and trying to get free. With a great effort he heaved Rhodes and Ruth backward and crawled off down the aisle.

Rhodes crawled after him. He caught him near the altar.

Barnes stood up, grabbed Rhodes by the shoulders, and threw him through the altar rail, which splintered as Rhodes crashed into it. Rhodes stopped rolling at the edge of the dais.

There was another shot, and this time there was the unmistakable sound of a bullet smacking flesh.

Little Barnes screamed something incomprehensible.

"Freeze, scumbag!" Ruth Grady yelled. "I mean it, sucker!"

Rhodes believed her. Evidently so did Barnes. He sat down on the floor and didn't move.

Rhodes got out of the hospital without any trouble, unless you counted the shaving of a patch of hair, the application of something wet and cold to his bare knot, and the pressing on of a bandage.

At least there were no stitches. The skin was broken, but the cut wasn't deep and there had been only a little bleeding. Most of the blood had dried in Rhodes's hair, matted it and clotted it. Most of it had come out with the shaving.

Little Barnes wasn't so lucky. Ruth Grady had shot him in the arm, right at the elbow joint, breaking all kinds of bones that Rhodes didn't even want to think about. The pain was no doubt considerable, but Barnes had made no sound at all since being put in the ambulance that Rhodes had called from the church. Barnes also had several pretty bad scratches on his face and hands from the leaves of the bushes where he'd been lying in wait for Rhodes.

The Reverend Funk wasn't so lucky either. He wasn't physically harmed, but Rhodes could tell that his psyche had taken quite a beating. He lived only a block from the church, and he had gotten there almost at the speed of light after Rhodes called him. He seemed to be in a sort of shock, shaking his head and saying "I can't believe it" over and over, a sentence he interspersed with remarks like "Not the rose window!'' which meant nothing to Rhodes but a lot to the Reverend Funk, to judge from his astonished and sad expression. Rhodes went outside to look at the stable damage with him, but forgot to ask if the beheaded wise man was Balthazar.

Rhodes did see two spare bales of hay behind the stable. Stacked one atop the other, they made a dark bulk that he had mistaken for Barnes. He also saw that by standing at the corner of the stable and looking around it he could see the spot where he and Ruth had been lying pretty clearly. Barnes had seen him slip away and guessed what he was up to. Well, it had turned out all right, except for a bit more damage to the property of the church.

When Rhodes left in the ambulance, the Reverend Funk was standing by the stable with his glasses in his right hand. His left hand was massaging his face. Rhodes wondered if he was praying or crying.

It was only seven o'clock when Rhodes left the emergency room. He had called Ivy to tell her that if he got by at all that night, he would be very late. He had also told Ruth Grady to get Buddy, the grappling hooks, and some lights and meet him at Little Barnes's well.

When he got there, the lights had already been set up on stands. Buddy and Ruth had not known exactly what was going on, but they had directed the lights at the well house.

It was cold, but not as cold as Rhodes had thought it might be, not freezing at any rate. Buddy had on an old coat that had sleeves about an inch too short. His shirt sleeves were caught back by the elastic in the coat, and his naked wrists gleamed whitely in the light. He was as tall and thin as the posts in Barnes's new corral.

Rhodes got out of his car and felt as if he were entering the set of a forties horror film. The cold air, the eerie lighting effects, the shifting shadows, all reminded him of *House of Dracula*, and he half-expected to see Lionel Atwill slink around the huge dark oak.

"It's a little dark for a rodeo, even with these lights,'' Buddy said. "I guess you got a better use for them.''

151

"Will those cables stretch from the battery over to the well?" Rhodes asked.

"I think so," Ruth said. She had her coat zipped up and looked smaller and more compact than usual. It was standing next to Buddy that made the effect work.

"Let's move them, then," Rhodes said.

"I guess I can figure it out for myself," Buddy said. "I'll get the grapplin' hooks."

They got two lights near the well housing, and Rhodes took the top off. All three of them peered down into the darkness.

All they could see was one of the lights reflected in the water fifteen or so feet below them. It was like looking at the moon in an icy lake.

"Who do we think is in there?" Buddy asked.

"Dr. Samuel Martin," Rhodes said.

"Did Barnes admit it?" Ruth asked.

"Not exactly," Rhodes said. "Let's get the hooks in there." He was ready to get it over with. The cold air felt even colder on the bare, shaved patch on the side of his head.

Buddy dropped the hooks down, letting the ropes slide slowly through his hands.

They heard the hooks splash into the water.

"Keep going," Rhodes said.

"How deep is this well?" Buddy asked.

"I don't know," Rhodes said. "Twenty feet? Twenty-five? Not too much deeper than the water, anyway."

Buddy continued to play out the ropes.

"Feel anything?" Ruth Grady asked.

"Nope," Buddy said.

"Keep going," Rhodes said.

"What makes you think he's down there?" Ruth asked.

Rhodes told them about the cement Barnes was using in the postholes, about Barnes's animosity toward Martin, about what happened when he confronted Barnes.

"But he didn't say he dumped him in the well?" Ruth asked.

"No," Rhodes said. "He didn't."

"Just as well," Buddy said. "He woulda been lyin'."

There's nothin' down there at the bottom of that well but a bottom."

"Are you sure?" Rhodes said.

Buddy handed him the ropes. "Give it a try for yourself," he said.

Rhodes pulled the hooks up, then lowered them. They went down smoothly, without a hitch except when he bumped them into the sides of the well. There was nothing to slow their progress in the least. Then they hit the bottom.

Rhodes pulled them up and tried again, with the same result. "Uh-oh," he said.

Back at the jail Rhodes was talking things over with Hack, who was of the opinion that they could convict Barnes anyway. "We got a motive," he said. "And we got Barnes's reputation. And we got the way he started in to shoot at you. I'd say he's a goner. Life for sure."

"Motive," Rhodes said. "He was just one of a lot of people who owed Martin money. So did Swan and Higgins, and I let them go. And Little's reputation isn't going to help us. How do you think most people on a jury feel about dentists? Probably half of them wouldn't mind whipping the one they go to, and they might think that if Barnes did it and got away with it, more power to him."

He put his hand to the spot on his head, which still sprouted a considerable knot. "The other half of them would like to assault me. Or some peace officer that gave them a ticket they thought they didn't deserve one time."

"Maybe the D.A. could work it out so the jury had just Presbyterians on it," Hack said. "Maybe he could get Reverend Funk to be the foreman."

Rhodes smiled at the thought. "They wouldn't put him *in* the jail," Rhodes said.

"They'd put him *under* it," Hack finished for him.

"That won't ever happen, though," Rhodes said.

"What about that case in Houston not so long ago?" Hack asked.

"Which case?"

"The one where the jury convicted that fella of murder

and there was no body. Not even much of a motive, if I remember rightly."

"I read about it," Rhodes said. "The prosecution had witnesses, though."

"Yeah, but not a one of the witnesses saw the murder. One of 'em saw something wrapped up in a sheet or a blanket that looked like it had blood on it, and one of 'em heard some shots. That was about all."

"I'd settle for that," Rhodes said. "I don't even have witnesses that good."

"They were all drug fiends, too," Hack said.

"If you believe the defense attorney," Rhodes said.

"Well, they got that fella anyway," Hack said. "I bet we could, too."

"We can hold him for assault with intent," Rhodes said. "That ought to go pretty hard on him, what with his past record, but it won't do a thing about Dr. Martin."

"What do you think about that?" Hack asked. "About Martin, I mean. You think Barnes did him in?"

"I don't know," Rhodes said. "I was convinced of it when he jumped me in front of the drug store. It just didn't seem like there could be any other reason. Now I don't know. I'll have a talk with him tomorrow and see where it leads."

"What about Miz Martin?"

"I thought he was good for that one, too," Rhodes said. He got out of his chair and walked over to the Christmas tree, looking down at the presents. There still wasn't one for Ivy under there. Or for Ruth. "I could see Barnes and his old mean daddy thinking that since the husband was dead, the wife would be easy pickings."

"I can see that myself," Hack said. "Too bad it won't work out that way in the end."

"It still might," Rhodes said.

"How's that?" Hack asked.

"I'm not sure," Rhodes told him.

Chapter 18

THE NEXT DAY a south wind came blowing up from Mexico, and the temperature had already warmed up into the fifties by the time Rhodes got to the hospital. The humidity was high, and it seemed as if there might be more warm weather on the way, one last reprieve from winter before Christmas.

Little Barnes was in no mood for talking. The prospects were that he wouldn't be able to enjoy the weather because he would be either in the hospital or in jail. Neither idea seemed to make him very happy.

"I got nothin' to say," he told Rhodes. "I want to get me a lawyer."

"That's fine with me," Rhodes said. He looked around the hospital room at the vinyl-covered furniture, the plastic water pitcher and glass on the cheap bedside stand, the tiny television set on its perch on the wall. "Sooner or later, you're going to have to talk to me."

"It'll be later, then," Barnes said. His arm was in a cast, a fact that probably added to his unhappiness. It was doubtful that he would ever have full use of it again, the flexibility being impaired permanently.

"You know I'll be filing on you for assault," Rhodes said, his hand going to the bump on his head. The swelling had decreased some, but it was still tender.

"I been there before," Barnes said. He looked out of place in the cranked-up hospital bed. He was so big that the bed looked like a child's bed. He was covered with the sheet, but Rhodes couldn't help wondering what he looked like in his hospital gown. Those gowns did a pretty inadequate job of covering a normal-sized person, or at least that had been Rhodes's experience. He figured that the nurses had gotten a few good laughs at Barnes's expense.

"I looked in your well," Rhodes said. "I thought I might find somebody there."

"Ha!" was all Barnes had to say about that.

"I'd still like to know what caused you to act the way you did," Rhodes said.

Barnes didn't say anything.

There was a telephone on the bedside stand, one of the old-style black ones that you seldom saw anymore. Rhodes put out his hand and touched it. "I'd give that lawyer a call if I were you," he said. "I think you're going to need him."

After leaving the hospital Rhodes drove around awhile to think. He was sure that Swan and Higgins weren't guilty of anything more than being a little strange—at least for Blacklin County—and a little behind in their rent. If they had lived in San Francisco, they might just have been behind in the rent a bit and a lot less strange.

And Barnes was going to deny, deny, deny. He couldn't deny the fact that he'd jumped Rhodes when the subject of Dr. Martin had been brought up, and he couldn't deny that he'd run away. He also couldn't deny the shots he'd fired or the kidnapping of Rhodes.

Kidnapping. It was a word that had just popped into Rhodes's mind. Was it possible to get Barnes up on kidnapping charges? That was an avenue worth considering.

So who did that leave? Among the possible suspects that

156

Rhodes had considered, it left only one. He headed in that direction.

The apartment house was quiet, most of the residents having gone to their jobs and dropped the kids off at the day care center. Rhodes parked and walked to the door of Carol Shamblin's apartment.

He knocked. There was no answer. Rhodes looked around the apartment parking lot. There were only a couple of cars there besides his own. The sun sparkled off the bumper of a Ford Escort.

Rhodes knocked again, a little harder.

"It's open," someone said from inside.

Rhodes turned the doorknob and gave a push. The door swung inward.

The room was almost exactly as Rhodes had seen it previously. Nothing seemed to have moved. Carol Shamblin sat on the same cheap couch, and she was wearing the same maroon robe. The robe was a lot more wrinkled than it had been. There was a blue haze in the room, and smoke circled the light of a small lamp, the only light in the room.

Even the stack of newspapers was there, if a little messier. The ashtray was overflowing with cigarette butts. There were even butts in the cup and saucer on the coffee table.

Rhodes walked over to the chair where he'd sat before. Carol Shamblin's eyes followed him.

"I thought you'd be back," she said. There were dark circles under her eyes, dark as bruises. Rhodes wondered if she'd left the chair at all since he'd been there.

"It took me awhile to figure things out," Rhodes said. He sat in the chair. "You want to tell me about it?"

"Not particularly," Carol said. She leaned forward and picked a cigarette butt out of the saucer and held it up to look at it. There was maybe a half an inch in front of the filter.

"I thought you might want to," Rhodes said.

"Well, I don't," Carol said. She knocked a little of the burned end off the butt and lit it with the green Bic, which she took from a pocket of her robe. She inhaled smoke. "How'd you figure it out?" she asked, letting smoke out of her mouth as she spoke.

157

"Process of elimination," Rhodes said, hoping that sounded scientific and accurate instead of as haphazard as it had actually been. "When all the suspects are eliminated, the one that's left is the guilty party."

Carol took another drag on the cigarette, then crushed it out before smoking the filter. "So you thought it might be someone else at first?"

"That's right. You had me fooled."

Carol leaned back on the couch. She seemed at ease for the first time since Rhodes had met her. The release of tension did that sometimes.

"I wasn't trying to fool anyone," she said. "It was just something I couldn't talk about. I . . . I didn't mean to do it."

Rhodes wished he had a nickel for every time he'd heard that line, but it was probably the truth. Most people did the things they did without thinking of them, whether it was driving too fast or running over the neighbor's dog. "I'm sure you didn't," he said.

She looked at him, the circles under her eyes seeming to darken. "You don't have to be condescending. I'm telling the truth."

"I believe you," Rhodes said. He wanted to keep her talking, to get her to tell how she did it. Mostly he wanted to know where Martin's body was.

She put an arm up on the back of the couch. Rhodes noticed again how large and strong her arms looked.

"Maybe I did mean to," she said. "Maybe what I should have said was that I didn't *plan* to. It was just something that happened."

"Because he wouldn't go away with you?" Rhodes asked.

"I guess that was it. I was pretty hurt." She looked in the ashtray for another butt, found one, straightened it a little, and lit it. "I was foolish, of course. I should have known that he didn't mean it."

She'd been thinking, which was a good sign. Probably her thoughts had run along the same lines as Rhodes's. Where could they go? Why leave a good practice and try to begin

158

over? And how could you begin over if you were a dentist? It wasn't like working at a service station.

"I don't blame you for being hurt," Rhodes said. "Did he tell you why he wouldn't go away?"

"How could he?" Carol asked. "I haven't seen him."

Rhodes didn't say anything. He was too surprised. Here he was, thinking that someone sitting not ten feet from him was confessing to a crime, and being completely fooled. Suddenly the air in the room seemed too close. The smoke seemed to seep into his lungs all at once, and he had an almost overwhelming desire to cough.

"Do you think he'll come back?" Carol asked.

"I . . . uh . . . I don't know," Rhodes said, being completely honest. He not only didn't know that, he didn't know what was going on at all.

"Do you think he'll speak to me?" Carol tossed the butt into the coffee cup, where it smoldered briefly, sending up a thin white line of smoke. "I don't mean see me again. I guess I couldn't expect that. I mean just speak to me. Be nice to me."

"Well . . . he might," Rhodes said.

Carol leaned forward suddenly, speaking intently. "He ought to," she said. "It's just as much his fault as it is mine. If he'd just come by, it wouldn't have happened. I think it was all the business with the curse. It got him so upset. I told him to forget it, not to even call you. But he had to do it. He thought that woman was crazy. If it hadn't been for that, he might have done it. He might have gone away with me. It's all that woman's fault."

Rhodes didn't think this was the time to tell her that the woman she was so upset with wasn't a woman at all. "We can't always blame someone else," he said. "Sometimes we have to take the responsibility for our own actions."

Carol relaxed and leaned back again. "You're right," she said. "I know that. But still, if everything hadn't gone wrong, I wouldn't have killed her."

This time it was Rhodes who sat forward. " 'Her'?" he asked. "You killed Mrs. Martin?"

"Of course," Carol said. She looked puzzled. "What have we been talking about all this time?"

Rhodes got Carol to the jail and Lawton installed her in the cell previously occupied by Betsy—or Barney—Higgins. Ruth Grady searched her without making any startling discoveries.

"So she killed Miz Martin," Hack said. "I always say, you never can tell about a woman."

Ruth Grady had gone back out on patrol, so no one bothered to contradict him. Lawton, in fact, shook his head in agreement. "Hell hath no fury," he said, as if it was something new.

"She didn't mean to do it," Rhodes said.

"That's what they all say," Hack said, echoing Rhodes's own thoughts.

"I mean she really *didn't* mean to do it," Rhodes said. "She just went over there to see if Martin was there, and maybe to ask him what was going on. When she saw that his Suburban was gone, she got out and went to the door. That was her big mistake."

"Not to mention it didn't do Miz Martin any good," Hack said. "What did she do, coldcock Miz Martin right then and there?"

"No," Rhodes said. "I gather there was quite a discussion, though, what with Miz Martin knowing about Carol and Dr. Martin and their little romance. She accused Carol of first one thing and then another, and Carol must have called her a few things too."

"Catfights," Hack said. "I remember I had to break one up one time. Worst I ever got hurt in my life. When two women get goin', you better just back off and get out of the way."

"I think this one was mostly words," Rhodes said. "Sort of hot, but not physical. But sometimes words can hurt worse than anything."

"You got that right," Lawton said, joining in. Then he thought about it. "Except it wasn't words that caved in Miz Martin's head."

160

"It was words that caused it to get caved in," Rhodes said. "I think Mrs. Martin called Carol a low-down, husband-chasing, lying bitch. Or something pretty close to that. Then she gave Carol a little push toward the door. That must have been something, that little woman pushing that big one. Maybe it was the push that did it. Some people don't like to be touched like that."

"I don't," Lawton said, "but I don't think I'd kill somebody for doin' it to me."

"You've got to remember that both of them were under a lot of strain," Rhodes said. "That can make a difference."

"Some people can get under a strain if they don't get a nice present for Christmas," Hack said, looking meaningfully at the small tree.

Rhodes ignored him. "Anyway, Carol went outside, getting madder by the second. She saw that toolbox in the garage, with a crowbar sticking out, and that was that. She grabbed it up, went right back in the door, caught up with Mrs. Martin, and clobbered her with it. That's all it took. She was mad, and she was strong."

Lawton leaned back against the door frame. "She was pretty smart, too."

"Yeah," Hack said. "She must have come to her senses pretty fast."

"I guess she did," Rhodes said. "But I should have known from the start that it wasn't a real burglary. Not enough things taken. Lots of stuff scattered, but not much really missing."

"What'd she do with it?" Hack asked.

"It was in the backseat of her car," Rhodes said. "Covered up with a blanket. The crowbar, too. Been there all the time."

"Smart, but dumb," Lawton said.

Rhodes frowned. "Hard to say. It might've worked, but I don't think she even wanted to get away with it. I think she was just running on automatic pilot after she hit Mrs. Martin. In shock, maybe. Trying to do something to muddy the water, but not trying to get away."

"You think she did in Dr. Martin, too?" Lawton asked.

"I don't think so," Rhodes said. "If she did, why con-

161

front his wife and have an argument about him? It wouldn't make sense."

Hack pushed back in his chair and put his feet up on his desk. "None of this whole thing makes sense. Right from the first, it was crazy, with that curse and all. I wouldn't be surprised if it was the curse that did it, myself. That Higgins fella—or whatever—is the guilty one."

"When you think about it, you might be right," Lawton said. "That's what got everything stirred up."

"If they hadn't called the sheriff about it," Hack said, "none of this would've happened."

"I don't believe in curses," Rhodes said.

"Where's Martin, then?" Hack said.

"I don't know," Rhodes told him.

Chapter 19

RHODES SPENT THE REST OF THE DAY on paperwork and in visiting Little Barnes in the hospital, this time with Barnes's lawyer present. The lawyer was Wally Albert, a mild-faced, pleasant man who looked more like a college professor than a lawyer.

"My client prefers that I do the talking for him," Albert said, his eyes sparkling behind his glasses. Rhodes could tell the lawyer was already having fun, and the game had just begun.

"That's all right with me," Rhodes said. "What does he want you to say to me?"

"He wants me to say that he has been treated shamefully by you and your department," Albert said, the mildness disappearing from his face as if it had never been there, revealing the toughness it had hidden. "He is considering bringing suit against you for brutality. After all, you beat him savagely and endangered his very life."

Rhodes was tempted to say that Barnes had started it, but that seemed too childish. "I just stopped by his truck to ask him a few questions," he said. "He fled the scene, and I considered him armed and dangerous."

"You sound like a police report, Sheriff," Albert said.

Barnes nodded approvingly from the bed, but said nothing.

"I suspected him of involvement in a crime," Rhodes said. "His behavior seemed to indicate that he might very well have guilty knowledge. And then he shot at me."

"Ah, but you were brandishing your pistol in his face," Albert said.

Rhodes wanted to tell Albert that his mother wore army boots, but he thought better of that one, too. He could see that the discussion could easily degenerate into a "Did not"/ "Did so!" argument if he didn't control himself. Lawyers didn't bring out the best in him.

"Does he have any witnesses to that effect?" Rhodes asked.

"Ah, well, for the moment, that will have to remain our little secret," the lawyer said.

"That's fine," Rhodes said. "On the other hand, I don't mind saying that Billy Lee down at the drug store saw the whole thing through his plate-glass window, and he'll be glad to testify to that in court." In fact, Rhodes hadn't spoken to Lee, but he was sure that Lee had been watching. At least, he hoped so.

"Mummmmmm, yes, well, be that as it may, we don't know what it is that Mr. Lee saw, do we?"

"I don't know about 'we,' " Rhodes said. "*I* know what he saw. He saw that I didn't take out my pistol until your client had run away, not until 'way after I'd been pushed into the street. Did I mention, by the way, that I think your client might be guilty of kidnapping?"

"Uh, no, I don't believe you did."

"Well, I do." Rhodes looked at Barnes. "You might be better off if you can get him to tell you things a little straighter, Wally. See you in court." Rhodes pulled open the door and went out into the hall. He listened to the door sigh shut behind him, hoping to hear a word or two of lawyerly conversation as well, but no words escaped.

164

Rhodes walked down the hall and went outside. It was four o'clock, and the weather had stayed warm. Rhodes wondered if he had time to go fishing. He was convinced that Barnes was guilty, but there was nothing more he could do with him for the time being. Let him stew a little. Worry him a bit with the kidnapping threat. Then Rhodes could try him again. Give it twenty-four hours.

Rhodes drove to his house and got his spin-cast rod with its Zebco 33 reel. He had an extra, so he called Ivy at work.

"Want to take off early and go fishing?" he asked.

"I guess I can," she said. "Who's buying the bait?"

"We'll just cast a little," Rhodes said. "I'll bring my spare rod and reel. Five minutes?"

"I'll be ready," Ivy said. She worked at an insurance office, and Rhodes thought it would be all right if she took some time off. Her boss liked and appreciated her, and he wouldn't begrudge it.

Rhodes hunted up his tackle box and tossed it and the two rod-and-reel combos into the back of the county car. This wasn't official business, but he didn't think the commissioners would complain. He was going to visit the site of a suspected crime, after all.

He picked up Ivy, who was waiting in front of her office. She was wearing low heels, but her pants outfit was much too nice to go fishing in. Or most women would have thought so. "I don't need to change," she said when she got into the car. "We don't have much daylight left."

Rhodes knew that he wasn't making a mistake in being engaged to her. Anyone who understood the importance of fishing was a rare treasure.

"Where are we going?" she asked.

"I thought we'd run out to Little Barnes's place. Or Dr. Martin's. Little told me the other day to come on out, and Dr. Martin isn't in any position to object. I wish he could object, to tell the truth."

Rhodes had told Ivy the whole story the night before after finally leaving the jail. She reached out and touched the patch on his head. "Are you sure you feel like fishing?"

Rhodes was surprised. "It doesn't bother me at all," he

said, and it was the truth. In fact, he hadn't even thought to mention it to Wally Albert, who was sure to have noticed it.

When they got to the Barnes place, Rhodes stopped at the gate. Ivy got out and opened it. It wasn't really a gate, just a gap in the barbed wire fence that opened back. Anybody who could open one as easily as Ivy did was deserving of praise. Rhodes usually couldn't get the wire that held the gap together to come apart, or to slip up over the post, whichever was necessary. He drove through, and Ivy closed the gap. Then she got back into the car.

They drove to the stock tank. The wooden dock Barnes had built for fishing extended out into the tank for twenty feet or so. The planking had weathered a uniform gray. Sitting on one side of the dock was a ceramic or chalk statue of a black man, who was holding a fishing pole. Rhodes decided that the statue was probably Barnes's idea.

He stopped the car under a large mesquite tree, hoping he hadn't driven over any of its branches. Mesquite thorns could puncture a tire as quickly as a nail, and they sometimes lay in wait when rotten branches fell off the tree. A tree as old as this one was likely to have shed a branch or two sometime in its history.

Rhodes got the rods and the tackle box out of the backseat, and he and Ivy walked out on the dock. "Left side or right side?" he asked.

"Left," Ivy said.

"H & H?"

"If you have one with a black and yellow tail," Ivy said.

"That's the only kind I have," Rhodes said. He took two of the spinners out of the tackle box and handed one to Ivy. She took the rod leaning against the left side of the dock, opened the swivel at the end of the line, and attached the spinner. Some people—purists, Rhodes thought—like to tie their spinners on. He'd never seen the sense in it. He caught plenty of fish this way.

They cast for a few minutes in silence, aiming for sticks or weeds that poked through the top of the water. Rhodes liked to fish in clear water when he was using artificial baits,

166

but this tank was fairly muddy. He hoped the noise of the vibrating spinner blade would attract a bass.

He was about to say something to Ivy when the tip of her rod dipped and she jerked back, setting the hook. "Got 'im," she said. She began to crank the reel, and the line ran out against the drag. She pumped the rod and cranked harder.

"Must be a big one," Rhodes said. He felt the excitement in his stomach that he always felt when either he or someone he was with hooked a good fish. "Keep him coming."

"He wants in those weeds," Ivy said, referring to a patch of greenish brown that stuck up ten yards from the dock.

"Don't let him get tangled in them," Rhodes said. He was thinking that it had been a long, long time since he'd fished and that the monofilament line might have gone bad. If the fish got in the weeds, he'd break it for sure. "Don't let him jump, either."

Ivy didn't say anything, concentrating on cranking and pumping. She got the fish to within ten feet of the dock when something happened. The fish had been coming smoothly, when suddenly it made a stop. Then it ran to the right. Then to the left.

Then the line parted as smoothly as if it had been cut.

"Damn!" Ivy said.

Rhodes was surprised. He'd never heard her say that before. "What happened?" he asked.

"The line broke," Ivy said, holding up the rod. Rhodes could see the thin, clear monofilament, limp and crinkled, lying on the surface of the brown water.

"It was like he ran into a wall," Ivy said. "I felt it. There's something in the water out there."

Rhodes looked at the water, but he could see nothing below the surface. There was too much sediment in the water. He cast his own spinner out beyond the place where the line had parted and reeled it back slowly. It bumped into something hard, then rode over.

"Did you notice anything before?" he asked.

"No," Ivy said, "but I might have been reeling faster than you were."

Rhodes looked at the bank near the place where the underwater object lay. He thought back to the previous evening and the grit in Barnes's pickup bed and the thick mud under the back wheel wells.

Sure enough, he could see the impressions of the tires in the soft mud where the water washed up on the bank. It was shallow and clear there, and a small school of minnows flashed through the tire tracks.

It was getting near to sunset, but with the humidity in the warm air, it felt more like springtime than winter. Rhodes knew, though, that the water would be cold. He walked down off the dock and looked for a limb from the mesquite tree. He found one about four feet long and thick as his arm.

"What are you doing?" Ivy asked.

"Just poking around," Rhodes said. He waded out into the water.

He was right. It was cold. It seeped through his shoes at once and soaked his socks. His pants legs clung to him with a clammy touch.

"Poking around?" Ivy said. "You must be crazy. Are you looking for the fish?"

"I'm pretty sure the fish got clean away," Rhodes said. "I'm poking." He gave a push at the water with the mesquite limb, feeling the rough bark turn in his hand.

The limb met something hard and solid. Rhodes tried to figure out its dimensions, then waded back to the bank. His legs and feet immediately felt wetter and colder out of the water than they had felt in it.

He stood for a minute letting the water drip down his legs and run out of his shoes.

"I can't believe this," Ivy said. "What on earth?"

"I'm wondering where we can borrow a tractor," Rhodes said. "And a long chain."

Buddy had the lights up again, but it was warmer than it had been when they had looked in the well. Rhodes had driven down the road to the house of Harmon Heyes and asked to borrow a tractor and chain. Heyes had provided both, along with a towel, but Rhodes was wet again.

He was wet all over this time, because he hadn't had an

easy time of attaching the chain to the concrete block in the tank. When it was finally done, Harmon Heyes cranked the tractor and moved off.

The block came out of the tank, sucking a little as it left the muddy bottom and stirring up mud and bubbles as it came.

When it was on the bank, they looked at it under the lights. It was wet and dark, about a foot and a half thick and about eight feet long.

"You think he's in there?" Buddy asked.

A bit of a breeze came by and Rhodes shivered. "I think he's in there, all right. I think Barnes built him a frame in his pickup bed and covered him in concrete and then dumped him in the tank."

"Pretty good idea," Buddy said. "Too bad he couldn't've got him into deeper water. We never would've found him then."

Rhodes got his towel and started drying off. He was sure he'd have a cold by the next day. He could already feel his sinuses acting up. "You never can tell," he said. "Ivy might have been fishing on the bottom for catfish."

"Do I get a Crimefighters' badge?" Ivy asked.

"No," Rhodes said, "but I might let you come to the jail Christmas party."

Rhodes was right on two counts. They jackhammered open the slab of concrete and found Dr. Martin. Rhodes also had a bad cold.

"Drixoral," Hack said. "I saw it on TV. Highly advertised stuff. Bound to be good for you."

Rhodes sneezed. "I don't believe in any of that stuff," he said.

"I didn't use to," Hack said. "But it may be better than what we used to have."

"Maybe I'll try it," Rhodes said. He knew he wouldn't.

"You talk to Barnes this mornin'?" Hack asked.

"Sure enough," Rhodes said. He sneezed again.

"You need to wash your hands a lot," Hack said. "I saw on TV that you can spread a lot more germs by touchin' things than you can even by kissin'. Not that you'd be doin' any of that. Kissin', I mean.''

Rhodes looked at him. Hack looked blandly back.

''What'd Barnes say?'' Hack asked. ''Better 'n that, what did old Wally Albert say?''

''Not much,'' Rhodes said. ''They can't seem to understand how that slab got in the tank.''

''Can you prove how?''

''Probably. We've got the tire tracks. We've got the concrete and the remains of it from Little's truck. We've got a motive that might look better with those things in mind.''

''How'd he die? Martin, I mean?''

''Don't know yet. Looked to me like he'd been hit. Barnes didn't know his own strength.''

''Still haven't been able to find anybody who saw him drive that Suburban out to Milsby?''

''Not yet,'' Rhodes said, sneezing one more time. ''Ruth's still asking.''

''I think we got him anyway,'' Hack said. ''You seen the mail?''

''You mean the invitation?'' Rhodes said. ''I've seen it.''

It was a wedding invitation, requesting Rhodes's presence at the uniting in holy matrimony of Marietta Ellen White and John Mark Stuart, the service to be held at ten A.M. at the Sunny Dale Home in room 121.

''You goin'?''

''Sure,'' Rhodes said. ''When is it?''

''Day before Christmas,'' Hack said. He looked over at their tree. ''They got a tree out there?''

''Not much of a one,'' Rhodes said.

''I was thinkin','' Hack said. ''Maybe we could share some of our presents with them out there. I hate to think of anybody not havin' a good time on Christmas.''

''I think that's a good idea,'' Rhodes said. ''Sometimes you surprise me, Hack.''

Hack didn't say anything. He kept looking at the tree.

''But we aren't going to share *two* of those presents,'' Rhodes said.

"Them two wrapped in the silver and gold foil?" Hack asked.

"That's right."

"I wondered why you was so late gettin' in this mornin'. You didn't spend all that time at the hospital with Barnes."

"That's right."

"You wouldn't want to tell me what's in 'em, I guess."

"Not me," Rhodes said. "That would spoil the surprise."

About the Author

BILL CRIDER is chairman of the English Department of Alvin Community College in Alvin, Texas, where he lives with his wife and two children.